Kitten

Leroy N. Smith

Contents

When recently broke, unemployed, and homeless Vika is given the opportunity to stay rent-free at her best friend's fiance's home, with the only condition being to take care of some pedigree cat, things are finally starting to look up. Even if Cleo, the cat, is a pretty poor conversational partner. And always seems to be judging Vika from a five-meter distance. Constantly. To an unfair degree, honestly. Either way, she's finally starting to get a handle of things.

Enter Noel. Doting owner of Cleopatra, and reserving all the same feline judgement, who immediately tries to pay her out of their lives.

Noel is something that Vika's pretty sure she'll never be able to handle.

chapter one

THE FIRST THOUGHT that crosses my mind when I see my mattress propped up against my front door is that I need to do laundry because wearing lacy underwear that rides up my ass is so unnecessary for a Monday night alone.

When I nudge the mattress over to uncover the doorknob to my apartment, my next thought is that I forgot to buy spinach for the salad I was planning to make.

I sigh, shrugging. Oh well. Chinese food it is. At least the black pepper beef comes with broccoli. It's green. That counts.

Creaking the door open, I'm immediately greeted by the musical styling of Rage Against the Machine, in all fuck-the-system type glory that is a telltale style Nikki is not in a good mood. I card through everything I could have done to cause it- left a mountain of unwashed dishes in the sink, borrowed her cute black dress without asking, or maybe she'd found out that I'd accidentally let her beta fish die when she was on vacation, and this one's just an imposter.

Either way, I probably deserve it.

Sucking my teeth, I step inside to the chaos, nose crinkling at the constant stream of clothes being hurled from my room into the kitchen. My clothes, particularly. With no proper care for their welfare, it seems, by the haphazard way they're being flung in the air.

Most of it's dirty, but I have a feeling that Nikki isn't helping me with laundry day.

I drop my oversized black purse at the kitchen counter, poking my head into my room where I can see a small Chinese girl fucking shit up in all definitions. Clothes are strewn everywhere, along with blankets, makeup, and basically everything that makes up my entire life.

"Now don't be alarmed, but I think we've been robbed, Nikki, and their signature is leaving mattresses outside in the hallway."

At the sound of my voice, Nikki freezes, head snapping at break-neck speeds to pin me down with a lethal glare and a homicidal sneer. She points an accusing finger at me. "You!"

I pause, pointing to myself. "Little ol' me?"

"You got fired!"

I blink, weighing my options carefully as I drink in the seething girl, her shoulders heaving, seemingly trying to murder me in my spot with sheer brain power alone. It's not a look I'm unfamiliar with, but it's still undeniably chilling.

I tilt my head and press a finger against my chin.

"Define what you mean by fired."

"Fired! As in, you no longer have a job. As in, you are unemployed. As in, you have no fucking means to pay me for three- yes, three months rent!" Nikki barrels past me, shoving me unceremoniously out of the way as she makes a quick getaway towards the living room. I escape her hell path and avoid getting mowed down, not that my safety is of any real consequence.

After I'd accidentally shattered her favourite mug and she'd thrown not one, but both her slippers major league baseball-style directly at my face, I'd learned not to get in the way.

"So is that a yes or a no for Chinese food?" I ask, stepping around the landmine of clothes and following her. Mostly because I don't trust her Hulk hands around expensive electronics, and it's Monday.

The television must remain in workable condition. Monday is Bachelor day.

With a frown punctuated on her face, she pauses next to the end-table, pressing a button into the machine found on top. A click sounds, and then I grimace as an irritatingly cheery voice breaks the rigid air.

"Hey Vika! It's me, Amanda, from work. Or well, ex-work I guess. I just wanted to say sorry about what happened, I know Garrison can be pretty tough, but it was pretty shitty of him to fire you on the spot last week. Even if you were sleeping on the job, but... anyways! I was just thinking, since I don't have your cell number, we should meet up again sometime! Get coffee or brunch something. Ring me back when have you have a second! See you soon!"

I restrain an eye roll, cursing myself for giving Amanda the landline number instead of my cell in the first place- usual practice whenever people are insistent on talking to me who I don't want to talk to. Like

Amanda, who, evidently, never knows how to keep her mouth shut about anything.

Nikki clears her throat, and I flash her a sheepish grin.

"Amanda's just crazy, isn't she? She's just lost it," I say, forcing out a nervous laugh, waving my hand like some PTA mom and pointedly avoiding Nikki's murderous stare. "So, shanghai noodles?"

"What's crazy is that you let yourself get fired for sleeping on the job. Is this a joke? Are you serious? Is this actually a goddamn joke?"

"What's a joke is that you still have a landline. Seriously, what century are we in?" I murmur under my breath, but despite the wailing sing-screaming that is blasting from the stereo, I can tell she hears by the sharp glare I get in response.

"Get out."

I swallow. "Nikki, listen, I'm being serious. Amanda really is crazy. After Doug left her, she's been totally off the rails. That'll happen to you when your husband leaves you for your own younger sister." I give a shrug in all who's-to-say fashion, batting my eyelashes in a way that I hope reads as innocent. "You can't really believe her, she's cuckoo."

That part's not a complete lie. Not getting fired totally is.

Nikki's lips press into a thin line, stare hardening. "I'm serious. Get out. I'm sick of this, I'm sick of you. I don't care anymore, okay? I don't give a shit that you're my cousin, you're family, whatever. You're out. Tonight. I'm serious."

"C'mon, Nikki, let's all be rational here. We're adults, we can figure this out-"

"What's rational is that you haven't paid rent in three months, and I already have someone that's moving into your room tomorrow. Someone with a job. Who can pay rent. An actual adult." She crosses her arms over her chest, dark eyes narrowed and lips pursed. She's radiating fury from every pore, a metaphorical fire burning around her.

"I'm an actual adult," I mumble, gaze falling to the floor. "It was just a shitty telemarketing gig anyway, and the boss was a creep. Now I can focus more on my bo-"

"Mention your fucking book, I dare you," she growls, holding up a threatening finger.

I throw my hands up in innocence. "Okay, just, give me a couple more weeks, I'll get you some money, we'll all be happy, it'll all be good. I promise."

She shakes her head, and for the first time since I've walked through the room, there's a tired stitch between her brows. "No, Vika, I can't do it anymore. I don't care what you do- but you're out. I mean it. Pack your things and go."

"What? Nikki, you're being crazy," I brush her off, rolling my eyes as I meander my way back to the kitchen where I'd left my purse. Digging through it, ignoring my dog-eared notepads and buttery bagel wrappers, I pick out my cellphone and shoot a grin at the incensed girl. "So, General Tso?"

"I will throw things at you," she warns, and it's less of a threat and more of a promise by the way her eyes darken, daring me to say another stupid thing.

I shift my weight, eyes darting to find an escape, waiting for the sigh of surrender that usually comes about this time. Usually. Today, her arms are crossed and defiant. I parch.

"Nikki, c'mon, where am I supposed to go? I can't go live with my parents because, oh yeah, they're dead."

She rolls her eyes. "Don't play that card."

"What card? The orphan card? The one you receive when you become an orphan?"

"Your parents died years ago and I won't feel bad for you right now- you got yourself into this situation. You're the one that dropped out of college, you're the one that got fired- no, I'm done. I called Natalya, she's gonna come help you get your things, because you're out, and I mean it- tonight."

Before another plea can leave my lips, she's stalking across the floor and slamming her door shut with a resounding thud.

I stand, shell-shocked for a moment.

No, this isn't supposed to happen. What's supposed to happen is sesame chicken and watching delusional, catty girls all vie for the attention of one obliviously stupid guy.

This cannot be happening.

I don't even realize that time has passed until a knock rips me from my reverie, and I shake my head, blinking as I return to the real world. Heavy guitar rifts are still humming in the air, and my stomach growls from the dying promise of Chinese food. Another knock and I sigh, crossing the room.

When I open the door I'm met with the soft green eyes and honey blonde hair of Natalya, a sympathetic crinkle in her brow. "I've been summoned."

I narrow my eyes. "She's not- she's not serious. She can't be. We're family. She's not kicking me out, don't worry, Nat. It's fine."

Nat scrunches her nose, lifting her cellphone with one hand and scrolling through the paragraphs of caps lock with her finger. "It seems like she's kind of serious, Vi. I think she specifically wrote that, yep, right there. I am fucking serious. Quote, unquote."

I shake my head. "No, no, she's not. She's just being dramatic. In a couple of hours, this'll all blow over."

The phone vibrates in her palm. "That is Nikki saying yes she is very serious, and that if I don't start helping you get your things like right now that someone's going to die. Wait! Also, she wants you to know that the person is going to be you."

Nat offers me a sympathetic smile, and I cast a sharp glare at Nikki's door. Mostly because I know she won't see it.

"I can't believe her," I huff, turning on my heel with a scowl marked on my face. "I even played the orphan card- the orphan card! How can she do this to me? We're family!" My voice rises a couple of decibels at the end, trying to get Nikki to hear, and she responds by turning the music up even louder. I groan.

"Well, she has been threatening to do it for the past couple of months," Nat murmurs, scratching the top of her head. When I shoot her a deadpan look, she claps. "But, I have a solution! It's- hey, Mark, you coming?"

I find myself less than surprised when Mark's grinning face appears in the doorway. He always seems to be only two steps behind at all times. The sleeves of his dress shirt are rolled up, ready for heavy lifting, and he gives me a friendly wave when our eyes meet. I smile back, because somehow Mark has this inane ability to look comfortable anywhere, even in this small grungy apartment, with a Rolex flashing on his wrist.

"I'm here to be used. Use me, please." He lifts his arms in open invitation.

Nat hides a smile behind her fingers. "I figured we could use some muscle."

I would vomit if they weren't genuinely adorable.

"Guys- it's fine. Really." I muster a reassuring grin, at this point trying to convince myself more than anything. "She's not really kicking me out."

Nat's phone vibrates, and she looks down. "Nikki says she's really kicking you out."

I swallow, stepping back to lean against the counter for support. My eyes trail over the apartment; the tiny little place I'd called home for the past two years. Countless memories were hidden within these four walls, seemingly an entire lifetime, even though I'd promised Nikki it would only be a couple of months when I first moved in. With one last wary glance at Nikki's door, I sigh in defeat.

"But I don't have anywhere to go." I'm rubbing my temples. "I'm gonna be homeless. I can't be homeless. I'm gonna miss the Bachelor. Homeless people can't watch the Bachelor."

Mark cocks his head to the side. "Aren't you more worried about food?"

My arms flail in the air. "That too! What am I gonna do?" I wail, pulling the skin of my cheeks with my palms.

From my peripherals I can see Nat roll her eyes. "You're always welcome to stay with me, I mean, I only have one bed, but we can make it work-"

"Really?" I gasp, relief crashing over me and a grin breaking out across my face. I look to her with hearts in my eyes. "You mean it? I promise I'll pay you some rent- I mean, when I get money. But I've got, like, things set up. So don't worry. Oh man, we're gonna be roomies!"

Just as I lunge to capture her into a death hold of a hug, Nat holds up a hand, stopping me. "Wait-"

"Wait?" I pout, freezing.

She snorts. "Trust me, you're gonna want to hear this. Okay, so Mark's roommate-"

"Mark?"

She shoots me a look.

"Right, not interrupting, because that would be rude."

There's a beat of silence where she narrows her eyes at me, then relents. "Right, as I was saying, Mark's roommate Alexei signed a lease with his girlfriend and moved out a couple of weeks ago, so you could potentially stay there? I mean, you'd have to move out before the wedding, but you wouldn't have to pay rent..."

"And I'm barely there anyways, Nat's place is way closer to my work, so I wouldn't be in the way," Mark adds, flashing me a reassuringly boyish grin.

I blink, taken aback. "Really, that's okay with you guys?"

Nat arches a brow. "What, should I be worried you're going to steal my man? Because I'd like to see you try."

A hand slaps over my melting heart, shoulders dropping with sincerity. "Oh my god, I love you guys. You guys are the best. You're better than any family I could ever ask for."

Nat's phone vibrates, and she checks it with a bemused grin. "Nikki says fuck you."

I brush it off, a mirage of my new, amazing life flashing before my eyes. I'd drunkenly crashed at Mark's before with Natalya, and despite only being a condo, his kitchen could swallow up my entire apartment. The words rent-free are still whispering sweet nothings into my ears.

"Oh, there's just one thing," Mark interrupts my thoughts, his blue-green eyes fixed on me.

A record scratches in my mind. "What?"

"I have a friend, and his cat- it's a long story, but she's staying with me right now. That all right with you? Are you okay with cats?"

I snort, brushing him off with a wave of my hand. That idyllic future crashes back in full technicolour. "Oh Mark, don't worry. Cats love me."

chapter two

THIS CAT DOES not love me. In fact, I'm pretty sure this cat hates me.

I sit on the countertop, swinging my legs as I hold my stare with the green eyes that have been relentlessly scrutinizing me for the past couple of days. Cold vanilla melts on my tongue as I narrow my gaze, hoping to evoke some sort of reaction from the cat, but nothing. Its expression never changes. Just pure, unadulterated contempt, as if I'm some vermin that's scrambled in from the outside. As if I should dare soil its gracious presence.

Quite frankly, this cat can fuck off.

"You're a cat. You don't get to judge me. You're basically a free-loader."

Nothing.

"And I worked on my resume today anyways. I'm going to get all of the jobs- watch me. I'm actually doing things. I'm not a freeloader."

Still nothing.

"Okay, so, I only changed one sentence, but the first step is the most important step. I opened it up on my computer. It's still there. It's only three. I've got the entire day."

Absolutely nothing.

"Oh, so you think 'cause you're one of those fancy cat breeds that has leopard spots that you're better than me? You're a cat. I'm a person. I'm above you."

Nothing.

"Fuck you."

Huffing, I jump off the counter, carefully cradling the tub of ice cream in my arms. For someone who barely sweeps through his own condo, Mark keeps the fridge surprisingly well-stocked. I'd barely left these walls in days.

Maybe a little too much indulgence, if the cat's judgement is anything to go by.

When my feet hit the tiled floor, the cat pads away to the opposite side of the room, maintaining the careful five-meter distance it's had since I got here. Which is all right with me, considering when I'd first arrived and tried to scoop dear Cleo up into my arms, the cat had done its best job to claw my eyes out.

Lessons have been learned.

I almost flip the cat off, and then realize that along with my little vacation, I'd barely made any human-to-human contact in a while, and that maybe I should do that, so at least I stopped looking to the cat for conversation.

I had gotten some headway on my book, not that anyone cared.

Stretching, I admit that I should probably do at least some of the job hunting I'd been constantly reassuring both Mark and Nat I'd been totally doing, and how dare they, I have definitely not been watching reality TV show re-runs all day.

Just as the thought crosses my mind, the doorbell resonates through the air, and I freeze.

Mark and Nat are both at some wedding cake tasting across town. For a moment I think it might be Alexei, Mark's old roommate, but he'd moved everything out weeks ago. I'm definitely not expecting any visitors.

The ending notes of the chime hang in the air for a moment as I look to the cat, who has made herself comfortable on the back of the couch. Our eyes meet. I blink.

"Are you gonna get that?"

Again, all the cat answers with is a glare.

I nod, sighing. "Right, yeah, I probably should do that. Expecting any deliveries? Doing a little late night shopping on Evil Cats 'R' Us?"

The cat does not appreciate my joke.

As I tread my way to the door, I catch a glimpse of myself in the mirror. My dark hair is pulled up into a ponytail, and there are remnants of mascara from when I tried to convince myself I'd actually be productive this morning. Wearing only some flimsy pajama shorts and an off-white t-shirt, that may or may not have some Cheeto dust near the bottom, I pause, wondering if this could be a problem.

Then I convince myself it's probably just some poor delivery boy that got lost and it'll be fine. Delivery boys have probably seen way worse.

When another knock sounds, I take another step, but just as I reach out for the doorknob, it jiggles. My eyes widen and dart around, looking for something to defend myself with.

I find only a spoon and the cat.

I'll probably just throw the cat.

As I gingerly take another step back, breath hitched in my throat, the door swings open.

It is not a delivery boy.

Instead, it's a man. His coffee dark eyes look down to meet mine, but I'm more focused on his sharp, tanned jawline, shaded with stubble, and those thick-rimmed glasses that seem to ignite every stupid tutor-student fantasy I've ever had. I swallow. The dress shirt he's wearing looks like it's never seen the threat of a wrinkle a day in its life.

Suddenly I'm very aware that the Cheeto dust is posing a much bigger problem.

He doesn't look like he wants to murder me, but as his narrowed gaze lands on me, I kind of feel like dying.

"Who're you?" he asks, thick brows knitted.

It takes everything inside of me not to run and slam the door shut in his face.

"Um, who are you?" I throw back, but it sounds too small, and I clear my throat after. "Can I help you?"

"Where's Mark?"

His intense gaze burns into mine, and I almost take a step back.

"Uh, Mark's not here," I offer lamely. "Sorry, would you like me to relay a message?"

The mystery man takes a moment to size me up, dark eyes rolling over my skin in a way that causes a fierce burning to crawl up my neck. I don't delude myself into thinking his curiosity is anything other than purely out of confusion, marked by the frown curved on his face. Still, I duck my head.

"What're you doing here?"

I take a deep breath, desperately trying to fight off a blush. "Right, yeah, sorry, actually um, so Mark and I are-"

"Mark and you?" he interrupts, brow arched.

I nod. "Yeah, Mark and I-"

Suddenly he's brushing by me, ignoring my half-human noises of protest. For a moment I'm trying to make sense of what the actual hell is happening, but figure at least if I'm murdered I'll never have to pay back Nat that fifty bucks I owe her.

"Sorry, excuse me, how rude of me not to invite you in," I murmur, mostly to myself.

He doesn't seem to care as he paces in the living room with a thoughtful grip on his chin. I wonder if I should offer him a drink or something, but then figure I don't really need to cater to a crazy person.

A good looking crazy person, but incapable of having a normal conversation nonetheless.

I look to the cat for help, but she's also totally ignoring me.

Worst guard cat ever.

Sighing in defeat, I slowly shut the door, turning to the new guest who's still pacing. "Sorry, can I help you? Like I said, Mark's not here, I'm not sure what you want me to do?"

He pauses at my voice, arms folded over his chest, still frowning. I sheepishly scratch the back of my head, unsure what to do with my hands.

"You need to leave."

I blink. "I'm sorry, what?"

He sighs, exasperated, running a hand through his dark hair. "I can't believe Mark would do this to Natalya. But- it doesn't matter now, you need to leave. Immediately. Get out."

I blink again, still confused, and a little off-put now. "Um... no?"

His eyes narrow as if he's surprised by my opposition. "You need to go," he says, matter-of-factly. "I can't believe he just let's you walk around here- God, he's so stupid. What if- either way, you need to leave. I'm serious. Go."

I bristle instinctively at being referred to like some untrained dog. "Listen, bud, I don't know who you are, but I have express permission from Mark to stay here, so let's calm down with your tone there. Maybe you should be the one to go, since you're the one that barged in here."

I poise a hand on my hip to try and look the smallest bit more intimidating in booty shorts. I almost want to throw some z-snaps his way, but then realize that middle school tactics might not work effectively against angry men in suits.

"You need to go," he repeats, again.

I shrug, mocking. "Well, I think you should go, so looks like we're at a stalemate, aren't we?"

I may be a freeloader, but I'm housebroken.

There's a beat of silence when his frown deepens, as if he could somehow look even more unimpressed with my existence. "I don't care about what he said, you need to be out. Now."

"I don't know how to tell you this, but I'm not-"

"How much?"

I pause, taken aback. "Wait- what? How much what?"

He sighs, as if I'm the one that's trying his patience, and reaches for a wallet in his back pocket. I watch with wide, curious eyes as he flips it open, thumbing through it. "Five grand? Is that enough?"

I tilt my head to the side. "Sorry- are you offering me five grand to leave?" I can't remember the last time my bank account even hit four digits.

He hesitates, cocking a pretentious brow in my direction. "Is that how to talk to you people?"

"You people?"

"Ten grand, then? Will that get you to leave?"

He pins me down with a dry look, pulling out a blank cheque and waving it in front of me.

There's a quick moment where I want to gape, indignant and tell him to less than politely fuck off, but then the numbers are still adding up in my mind and suddenly little dollar signs with wings are chirping before my eyes

I can't remember the last time I had more than a couple grand to my name, let alone ten. My mind wanders to the student debt still hanging over me, and my next-to-homeless living situation, and my recent unemployment, and any real dignity I had probably escaped the moment I made out with a taxi cab driver anyway.

Nat would understand. I'll buy her a nice purse and she'll be fine.

I clear my throat, squaring my shoulders and nodding, hoping to look as professional as possible in pajamas. "That's right- and I'm not taking anything less than ten grand. I am a woman of principle."

I am once again reminded of the Cheeto dust.

Something like Natalya's voice or a conscious is scolding me for scamming money from probably one of the wealthy guys that Mark plays golf with or poker with or whatever it is that rich guys do. Maybe I could, well, not.

But judging by the freshly polished Italian shoes, sleek leather wallet, and his tendency to just throw money at problems he's created in his own mind, it doesn't seem like he's hurting for cash. And for ten thousand dollars, I would happily end my freeloader life.

Everyone wins.

I can already picture myself throwing bills in the air, dancing around with my wads of cash like some low-budget off-label music video. I'm personally going to take pictures and send them to Nikki. That's what she gets for kicking me out.

"And how do you spell your name?"

My fantasy is broken by the mystery man, who's name I still have no idea. He's leaning over the kitchen counter, pen in hand, blank cheque ready, looking up at me with impatience. I beam.

"That would be Victoria, yeah, just like that, and then Phan, P-H-A-N, great, awesome." I'm leaning over his shoulder, a little too close it seems from the quick look of annoyance he throws me, but my greedy eyes are too busy watching him write more and more zeros on the line.

I can't wait to shove this cheque in that stupid cat's face.

"So you're going to leave, right? And never come back- I'm serious. This is a onetime fee, and I won't let it cash if I see you again," he says, holding the cheque towards me with skepticism drowning in his eyes. "I never want to see you again."

I beam back, quickly nodding my head and snatching the cheque from his hands. "Gone, forever, poof! You'll never see me again! Pleasure doing business with you!"

I reach out a hand, and he looks at it with narrowed eyes, mouth pressed into a thin line. I don't even care. I'm rich.

"Noel?"

As a new voice tears through the room, I jump, a little noise of shock escaping me. Mark stands in the doorway, confusion on his face. His eyes bounce from me to the man to me again, narrowing slightly.

"Mark!" I chirp, grinning sheepishly and quickly hiding the cheque behind my back. "What are you- uh, what's going on? Why're you here?"

"Nat forgot her wedding planner here, so I came back to get it," he explains slowly, eyeing me with suspicion. "What are you guys doing?"

The man, who I'm assuming is Noel, sighs next to me. "Don't worry, Mark. I took care of it for you."

"Yeah!" I agree a little too quick, eyes darting behind Mark to where I'd left my shoes. "Noel took care of it, so I'll just be on my way! Don't mind me."

With my hands still behind my back, I stealthily meander my way towards the door, the grin still frozen on my face. I realize that early spring weather isn't exactly booty short appropriate, but I'll freeze for ten thousand dollars. I can buy myself new pants. All I know is that I need to leave, judging by how Mark keeps looking at me, arms crossed over his chest.

Just as I brush by him and can taste freedom on my tongue, he plucks the cheque from behind me, and I jump.

"Mark!"

My eyes widen and zero in on the money, my future, held in his hands. The raining dollar bills dream. My breath catches at the back of my throat, and as I go to snatch it back, desperate, he holds it closer to him.

"What's this?" he asks, amusement reflected in his light eyes as he holds it above his head. "Is this a cheque?"

"Don't worry, Mark. Like I said, I took care of it for you. Let her go," Noel says, arms crossed over his chest, face still characteristically unimpressed.

"Yeah, Mark!" I huff as I jump and reach in vain for the cheque that's just inches from my grasp. I silently curse my height, or lack thereof. "He took care of it! Just! Give! It! To! Me!"

Mark smirks down at me.

Damn these tall men.

Still holding it above his head, Mark looks up, lips parting in shock. "Ten thousand dollars? Are you serious?"

Noel sighs, laced with exasperation, now seemingly annoyed with both of us.

I reckon he must be fun at parties.

"Mark- just let it go. I don't know what's going on between you and Nat, but you shouldn't succumb to this. I took care of it, so just let her go." Noel's still wearing this troubled look, as if he's some saint surrounded by idiots. I almost take offense to the way he refers to me as this, but I'm too busy trying to quickly grab my rightfully earned future from Mark.

"You think we're sleeping together?" Mark asks, way too amused for his own good.

My mouth twists into a scowl, and I point a threatening finger at him. "I swear to God, Mark, shut up and give me that cheque or so help me I will not stop sleeping with you," I murmur through clenched teeth, narrowing my eyes in a way that I hope reads as intimidating.

"Noel, I'm not sleeping with her."

Noel blinks, a wash of confusion over his face. "What?"

"He's lying!" I quickly burst out, flailing my arms in front of Mark. "He's lying to you! He's covering it up! We bang all the time!" I can't help the panic that bleeds into my voice, growing thicker as Noel's brows crinkle in thought.

Mark snorts, gently pushing my arms away. "You haven't met her yet, but this is Nat's best friend. She's just staying here while she gets back on her feet. Vika, this is Noel. Cleo is his, and he's gonna be my best man. Noel, this is Nat's maid of honour."

As Mark makes the introductions with a grin and sweeping arm gestures, I can see Noel's bewilderment quickly morph into a look of stone. I swallow, my eyes quickly flickering to the cheque still in Mark's hand. A myriad of decisions flash before my eyes.

Swiftly, I reach to grab the cheque from Mark's grasp, but he's quicker. With a disapproving look in my direction, he rips the paper in half, and then again, and again, until it falls in confetti to the tiled floor.

"No!" I wail, dropping to my knees and scrambling to pick up all the little pieces. "Mark! Why? Why would you do this!?"

Mark raises his brows at me, and even still, there's a sympathy reflected in his blue-green eyes. "C'mon, I can't let you steal ten grand from one of my best friends."

"Why not?" I moan up at him. "It's not stealing if he's just throwing it at me! Is it my fault? Really?"

Mark nods, a small smile on his face. "Yeah, I think it is."

With a pout, I lift to my feet again, sparing a longing glance at my murdered future. I never understood Mark's inane need to always do the right thing. Especially when it conflicted with my need of getting ten thousand dollars.

My eyes meet with Noel's, who's frowning again, a frequent occurrence if this experience is anything to go by. It's a shame with how well defined his jawline is that all he does is look like the world is constantly ending.

His gaze narrows. "I don't like to be made a fool of."

I shrug. "I don't like not getting ten thousand dollars. Looks like today isn't going well for anyone, buddy."

With one last sigh, I look to the shredded cheque. My best friend's face flickers through my mind.

"Hey Mark, you're not gonna tell Nat about this, right?"

chapter three

MARK TOTALLY TOLD Nat.

As predicted, she is not taking it well.

"Vika! Stop yawning! Mark's mom keeps looking over here!" Natalya chastises me in a harsh whisper, green eyes shooting daggers in my direction. Her hands are balled into fists on her lap, French tipped nails digging into her palms, and her glossy lips are pressed into a thin, no-nonsense line.

I cock an eyebrow, leaning back in my seat. "Is it a crime to yawn now, officer?"

The blonde girl pins me down with another murderous glare, communicating many a graphic threat on a non-verbal level. Her eyes carefully slide to the other side of the room, over to Mark's family- a litany of polo shirts, pearl necklaces, and roars of pretentious laughter. In the middle of it all is a woman who keeps throwing sharp stares in Nat's direction, artificially plumped lips pursed. I can't tell if it's intentional or just too much Botox.

I still don't understand how Mark keeps his Cocker Spaniel-like charm when everyone who genetically and circumstantially surrounds him are the most insufferable people. Other than Nat and I, of course.

Although, I'm not sure Nat would currently exempt me from that group.

"You watched a horror movie again yesterday, didn't you?" Her eyes narrow, and with a twinge of guilt I immediately start looking everywhere else but her face. She directs a quick kick under the table in my direction. "You know you can't sleep after watching them and you knew you had this today!"

I hiss, crouching over to protectively rub the inevitably forming bruise on my shin. "Oh, what, so rich people don't yawn now? You lose that capability when you think that paying fifty bucks for a couple leaves of lettuce is actually a good deal?"

"I'm going to murder you."

A cheeky smile touches my mouth. "In front of Mark's mom? What if you get blood on her ridiculous fur shawl?"

A look of horror passes over Nat's face as she pictures it.

This refers to what Mark and his family refer to as brunch, but I, who only woke up an hour before, am firmly calling breakfast. Nat had practically knocked the door off its hinges this morning, forcefully dragging me from the warm comforts of my blankets to the cruel, unforgiving, and most dreadfully cold floorboards. I barely had a grasp on reality before she was pushing me out the door, panic-stricken muttering about how Mark's mother hated people who are late.

She did not laugh when I said that Mark's mom hated pretty much anyone that didn't have a brick of solid gold shoved up their ass.

Despite the homicidal glares she's shooting me, we both know having a half-asleep Vika is better than having no Vika at all. When entering shark-infested waters, that is, brunch with the Vanderbilt family, there's strength in numbers.

Nat sighs, rubbing her temples with a tired look in her eyes. "Can you at least make nice with Noel? Mark's mom literally thinks he's the second coming, and my maid of honour trying to scam him of ten thousand dollars is not helping my case."

I roll my eyes. "One, I love Mark, but does he really need to tell his mom everything? Two, I did not scam him. I don't know why everyone keeps on making it seem like I did."

Nat arches a manicured brow at me. "Oh yeah, and what do you call tricking someone into giving you thousands of dollars then?"

"Is it my fault that he just barges into people's apartments and throws money at them? No, I think that's more his problem than mine. Everyone's criticism is a little unjustified here." I raise my brows, toying with the poor excuse of a salad that I paid way too much for.

When I meet Nat's eye, I can't help but laugh.

The beginning of the first genuine smile I've seen all day curve on Nat's lips, the suffocating atmosphere that the Vanderbilt's trail along wherever they go finally thinning. I can't help but note the man of the hour is with them too, sporting his usual frown.

When I look back to Nat, she's hiding a smile behind her hand. "He definitely thought Mark hired a sex worker."

"Honey, for ten thousand dollars, he can think whatever he wants of me."

A laugh escapes from the girl, and she immediately covers her mouth as if she hadn't been expecting it. Her green eyes are shining, and they playfully narrow on me as she leans back. "Well, go make him think that you're the most wonderful thing in the world, because I'm pretty sure Mark's mom is looking for any reason to call off the wedding, and Noel's hurt feelings might make that happen."

My eyes shift over to Noel, whose slight frown has upgraded to no expression at all, and he appears to be completely ignoring Mark's brother and sister in their attempts to pull him into conversation. With him distracted, I take a moment to absorb his dark hair and tall frame, thick-framed glasses perched on his nose and matching his black dress shirt, sleeves rolled up. I can't help but chuckle as Mark's younger brother claps Noel affectionately on the back, and his eyes widen, positively affronted.

"Who's this guy, anyway? I swear, he appears, and suddenly he's all I ever hear about," I muse, turning back to Nat, unable to tame the curiosity within me. "If he's so close with Mark, why am I just seeing him?"

It's a name I'd heard being tossed around here and there, more of a concept than a person, but it feels as if this guy's begrudgingly materialized from thin air looking for a way back to Kansas.

Nat shrugs. "Honestly, I don't know much about him either. He's been living in Hong Kong for the past four years, and now he's doing business here before the wedding. Apparently he and Mark have been friends since they were like, seven or something, and his uncle is some hotel tycoon that Mark's ad firm works for. But he's a total workaholic, which is why I think you've never met him before. Oh, and Cleo's his cat. That's literally all I know."

A sigh escapes my lips as my eyes are pulled back over to him. "You're saying that I pissed of Mark's richest friend? Really? I did that?"

Nat laughs. "Oh yeah, that guy's rolling in dough, apparently. You made a fool of the wrong guy."

She drops her voice a few octaves, but the grin that's smeared across her face betrays her Noel impression. I shoot her a dry look, and she opens her mouth as if she's about to make some smart remark back, but then her eyes fall over my shoulder towards the table with Mark's mom, and it dies.

"All right, all right," I sigh, throwing my hands up in surrender. "I already bought my dress so the wedding better not get called off. I'll go make nice with the best man."

Nat shoots me a small smile and I climb to my feet, forcefully pulling my lace dress down my thighs. Usually I opt for the shorter the better whenever I'm fraternizing with Mark's rich male friends, but I have a feeling that Noel isn't going to be impressed by some flashes of skin.

He's moved to the corner of the room, casually holding a scotch glass as he listens to Mark talk about something or another, looking like he's actually listening for the first time that day. Instinctively I pull my dark hair forward, preparing for what I know will be nothing short of the most awkward conversation I'll ever have.

And I've had a full conversation with my aunt over the phone in spread eagle.

"Fancy meeting you two here," I beam, sliding up next to Mark. "Hiding out, are we?"

Mark flashes me that boyish grin of his. "Seems we've been caught. But I guess I should go save my wife-to-be while I've still got one to save. If I leave her alone too long, she'll realize what a terrible mistake she's making."

I laugh as he shoots me a wink, and then Mark disappears across the room, next to Nat's side. The good-natured ambiance that Mark radiates quickly shrivels as I turn to Noel, whose subtle frown has returned with a vengeance.

"Hello," he murmurs, ice touching his words. I can see his grip tighten around his glass.

I grin, opening my arm towards him. "Hey! It's me, remember? Your favourite hooker!"

The only crack to his grim facade is a twitch of his brow.

"If we could forget about all that- that would be great." His eyes fixate to a potted plant in the corner

"Really? It doesn't seem like you've forgotten by the way you said hello."

His dark eyes steal mine and my smirk suddenly drops, an unfathomable shiver sparking down my spine. There's a quiet intensity smouldering in his pupils that robs me of my words.

"You're overfeeding Cleopatra."

At his voice, I'm blinking in confusion. "Wait- what? How do you know?"

"I can see the food bowl. She's going to get fat if you keep feeding her too much." That proverbial look of mild irritation flickers across his features.

I pause, an unsettling sensation overwhelming me. "You've been to the place?"

Suddenly I'm raking through my memories for any hint of his presence, any indication that he'd been around while I was belting lyrics in the shower, or loudly rehearsing conversations I would have with Nikki once I was a successful published author, or taking the Hitachi out for a little me time.

I parch. Or when I was telling his precious cat to fuck off.

He absently rubs his wrist. "Hmm, yes. Usually at night, so you were asleep. I have a key, remember?"

My shoulders immediately drop their tension. "Well, whatever. She looks at me and keeps meowing. What am I supposed to do?"

"She just wants attention, brush her why don't you? Isn't that supposed to be your payment for staying at Mark's place?"

I snort, crossing my arms over my chest. "Oh yeah, like I'm going anywhere near that demon cat."

I'm pretty sure that Cleo would be just as unimpressed with the thought of me going anywhere near three feet of her.

"Demon cat?" His brow creases, eyes widening a fraction.

"Yeah, you know, like a bloodthirsty demon creature that temporarily takes a feline form? Otherwise known as Cleo."

His gaze narrows into a glare. "It's Cleopatra, and she's not a demon." There's an undercurrent of venom in his voice, and it's the most emotion he's shown all day that surpasses mildly troubled or slightly confused.

I can't help the smirk that twitches onto my lips. "Her glowing red eyes beg to differ."

As he fixes me with another agitated look, I catch Nat's questioning gaze from across the room, and I throw a reassuring thumbs up in her direction. She narrows her eyes, suspicious as they trail towards the ever-frowning Noel. I purposefully step in her line of view to block him from the rest of the party.

"Could you stop looking like its the end of the world for like, twenty seconds? I'm not really that sorry, but if it's that important to you, I apologize for trying to accept a particular amount of money you were practically throwing in my face. All right? You good now? Truce?" I offer him a hand in all olive-branch fashion.

His eyes narrow on my outstretched arm, wary. There's a moment of quiet as I can practically hear the gears whirring in his head, probably trying to decipher what kind of poor-people disease he can contract from skin-to-skin contact.

Just as his mouth twitches, and he looks as if he's about to accept, there's a harsh whisper of my name in my ear.

Suddenly my mind is flooded with memories of last night, flickers of soulless eyes, translucent pale skin, and blood stained night gowns. My eyes widen in panic, and a small scream escapes my lips as I flail instinctively, already accepting my death via little ghost girl. My arms seem to move on their own accord, and my too-quick movements have the back of my hand shooting out and catching Noel's, specifically the one holding his drink.

The diamond-cut whiskey glass propels right into his solar plexus with a wince and an ooomph from the man himself. The who-knows-how-many-years amber liquid jumps from the rim to soak his shirt before all of it comes to kiss the floor in a deafening, splintered shatter.

Absolute silence floods the room. Forty pairs of eyes scorch into my back.

My eyes grow wide in tandem with the shock mounting in my stomach. When I throw a quick glance over my shoulder for good measure, it isn't a ghost girl at all. Turns out, it's just Mark's younger brother.

Close enough.

But the younger brother's usual smile is completely eviscerated, and as I follow his gaze back to Noel, I can feel a new kind of anxiety pinch at my heart.

I'm not sure assault is exactly what Nat meant when she told me to make nice.

"Oh my god," I gasp with my hands covering my mouth, shoulders tight with tension. "Oh my god, are you okay?"

When I catch his gaze, the chill that sparks down my spine is answer enough.

His arms are still frozen, open, and I can see his jaw flexing with exertion. Panic rips through my veins as he glares at me through his glasses, a sneer twisting on his mouth. "Do I look okay?"

I wince, sucking my teeth. "Um, yes?"

He doesn't even entertain me with a response.

"Ah, shit, I'm sorry. Really. I just, I was watching movies last night, so I'm a little jumpy. And it's also partially Mark's brother's fault for trying to scare me. Let's not forget about that. Anyways, let me help."

I drop down to a crouch, brows furrowed as I take in the fragmented mess that's overtaken the tiled floor. My hands hesitate as I try to find the most substantial piece in the sea of shards. With a hard swallow, I look back up to Noel to find him examining the damage of his god-knows-how-expensive button-up shirt.

I wince. "Sorry man. Hey, while we're still on the topic though, that truce, that's still on the table?"

His gaze shifts to mine in a murderous glower, and I throw my hands up in surrender, nodding in understanding. Maybe another time.

"Get up," he snaps. "You're going to hurt yourself. Don't touch anything."

I wave him off. "No, no- I can help. I promise. Just, uh-"

My voice trails off as I'm still crouched, still unsure of even where to begin. Never being born sounds like a great place to start.

"Go before I call my lawyer."

The word is still lingering in the air as I shoot up. "Lawyer?" I echo, softer.

Again, his answer is all in the eyes, narrowed and pinning me down. I grin sheepishly in reply, pointedly avoiding everyone's pervasive stares as I back away slowly and then make a sharp break for it.

Back at the table, Nat's green eyes are wide. She watches as I quickly collect my jacket and purse, my legs already buzzing with the need of escape.

"Where are you going, Vika?" she asks, bewildered.

I shoot her a strained grin. "Well, it seems I'm about to get sued for more money than I could ever imagine, so I'll be in the parking lot full of Teslas that are begging to be jumped in front of."

chapter four

THE GET-RICH-OR-LITERALLY-DIE-TRYING-PLAN, like most things in my life, falls short.

Nat had patiently reassured me that, to her knowledge at least, Noel is not planning on suing me. Although I'm pretty sure she only said that because I was two seconds away from throwing myself in front of a flashy Mercedes Benz. And that would probably look bad in front of Mark's family.

Which means to say, I've been left with all my limbs still attached, but also still dreadfully poor.

I haven't heard from the frowning man since. The grapevine- Mark- tells me Noel's busy and that's why I haven't seen him around. Extrapolating from the tone of voice Mark used, I'm not under the impression that Noel particularly cares about my totally sincere apology.

But none of that means anything now. Judging by the terrifying noises coming from outside my door, I'm pretty sure I'm going to die.

"Vika, it's one in the morning, I swear if this is about your book, I'm going to punch you in the face," Natalya groans through the receiver, sleep thick in her voice in a way that softens the threatening edge.

I don't have time for unimaginative insults about my novel. This is a matter of life or death.

"Is Mark with you right now?" I ask, eyes wide and trained on the door. "Yes or no, I need to know."

"Hmm? Yeah, why? Can I sleep now?" she mumbles, and from what I hear, buries her face into a pillow.

Ignoring the chill that sparks down my spine, I slowly lift the covers off of my body, goosebumps rising over my skin. I gulp when my bare feet touch the wooden floorboards and the hairs on the back of my neck stiffen. When I gingerly step closer towards the door, the voice from the television gets sharper

My pulse quickens.

"There's someone in the house," I whisper harshly into the phone. "Or something."

"You're overreacting, I'm sure it's just the cat."

I narrow my eyes, warily grasping the doorknob. Flickers of masked murderers and vengeful spirits cross my mind. "I'm sorry, last time I checked, cats can't turn on televisions, so there is clearly an intruder who wants to murder me and they're inside the house."

Nat yawns. "Cool, can I hang up now?"

"No!" I gasp, horrified. "Does my death mean nothing to you?"

"At one in the morning, no, not really."

My face drops. "All right, fine, just stay on the phone with me while I check it out. And make sure you're ready to call 911 if anything happens, okay? I'm serious. Promise."

I roll my eyes as she makes another noncommittal hum of confirmation, and my ears adjust back to the voices on the other side of the door. I'm not sure what kind of murderer would go through the trouble of turning on the television, but I'm not in the mood to psychoanalyze some homicidal maniac.

When I finally push the door open with bated breath, nothing immediately jumps out to murder me. With a hard swallow, I poke my head out into the darkness.

Shadows touch everything I can see, and from my angle, the living room is just out of view. Other than the distant voices from the television, there's quiet distilled in the air. When I take a cautious step forward, there's still nothing.

Suspiciously nothing.

With quick and light steps, I make a detour to the kitchen, hoping not to announce my presence to any would-be murderers. Unfortunately, when I pull open the drawer to arm myself, all that stares back at me are an abundance of blunt spoons. My eyes slide over to the dishwasher that, to my demise, is filled with all the sharp objects in the near vicinity.

I grab the closest thing to me that has any swinging power whatsoever- a ladle- and courageously trek to the living room.

When I stick my head around the corner, I'm met with the sight of the television, on, and silhouetting a figure on the couch. As my wide eyes land on the back of the perpetrator's head, my heartbeat trips, and my breath sharpens in a quiet gasp.

I almost say I told you so to Nat, but then I realize I told you so also means certain death for me, and I quickly shut up.

I nestle the cellphone between my shoulder and ear, gaining a better, two-handed grip on the ladle. My stomach knots tight, and as I take a few slow steps forward, my pulse thuds in my ears.

Just as the muted light of the television glints against the metal ladle positioned high in the air, the assailant turns.

"Christ, what the fuck are you doing?"

I scream.

My cellphone tumbles to the ground with a sharp crack, and I jump back, heart leaping up into my throat. Eyes the size of saucers, I look to the familiar man in front of me, dark hair, thick-frames, and all.

Chest heaving, I slowly lower my weapon. "What are you doing? It's one in the morning!"

His eyes narrow on the ladle. "Were you about to attack me? With that? That was your plan?"

He's donned in the usual pressed dress shirt and pants getup that I literally can't imagine him without, Cleo resting peacefully in his lap. The cat barely acknowledges my presence, and Noel continues threading his fingers through her spotted fur as he arches an eyebrow at me.

"You can't come into people's houses in the middle of the night!" My brows furrow, and I press a hand across my uneven heartbeat.

"That's not a normal thing to do! I'm not sure why I have to explain this to you!"

He fixes me with a sober stare, and a sense of realization seems to cross over his features. "I wanted to come to see Cleopatra after work. Did I wake you? Sorry about that."

Somehow I'm being engulfed by his painfully earnest face and then I'm the one giving a half-hearted grumble of reassurance that no, it's fine, so, whatever. My eyes fall everywhere but his, and then a thick silence settles over us.

I slowly reach down to retrieve my abandoned phone, which is thankfully intact. My thumb slides over the glass screen with relief. When I bring it back to my ear and call Nat's name, purposefully turning my body away from Noel, all I receive are quite snores in response.

"I could have died, Nat. I want you to know that. I could have died."

She, of course, says nothing back.

With a tired sigh and a roll of my eyes, I click the phone off and slip it into the pocket of my pink pajama shorts. When I turn back to Noel, he's no longer concerned with my existence.

His eyes are trained on the television screen and he's still lacing deft fingers through Cleo's fur. With him being painfully overdressed and me being painfully underdressed in a soft blue tank top, I almost feel a pinprick of embarrassment.

Then I remember I can't worry about any respect being lost when he literally had none for me in the first place.

And so I collapse on the couch, dropping the ladle beside me. "So, what are we watching?"

He shoots me a confused glance. "What? You can go to sleep. I said sorry about waking you up. Don't mind me."

I flash him a bright smile. "I was awake, so you're fine. I usually write in the night anyways," I admit, eyes falling onto the screen and somehow not being surprised at all to find an Australian accent narrating about the depths of the Amazon rain forest, because of course even his TV is educational.

He blinks, head tilting ever so slightly. "You write?"

A warmth blossoms in the pit of my stomach at the surprising lack of judgement in his tone. "And you thought I was some lazy freeloader," I say, jabbing an elbow in his direction.

"Let's not get too ahead of ourselves."

"Noel!" I gasp, shifting closer to him, which he notes with a narrow of his eyes. "And I thought we were getting to be good friends. After everything we've been through?"

The dry look he pins me with communicates exactly what he's thinking.

"Okay, before with the drink- I'll admit, my body may have overreacted slightly, and I'm sorry. But this time, you broke into my house at midnight, so almost attacking you I think is a little justified."

I cross my arms over my chest, and try to return the same amount of pretension back at him, but it hardly works. His eyebrows alone are on a whole other level.

"I have a key, I told you," he murmurs under his breath, eyes focusing on the screen.

"And I have a ladle."

His gaze drags over to me. "Are you threatening me?"

"All I'm saying is a heads up would've been nice. I take my self defence very seriously." I shrug.

"I'm aware."

A snicker escapes my lips, which I clamp my hands over too late. His eyes are saturated in contempt.

"Oh come on!" I blurt out through my laughter. "It wasn't even that bad, plus, I was just giving you a reason to take off your shirt and look awfully cool in front of everyone. I actually did you a service."

He frowns. "I'm not some exhibitionist."

"Listen, if not for you than for Mark's fifteen-year-old cousin. She'd been eyeing you all morning with hearts in her eyes. I'm giving the people what they want, Noel."

His lips thin. "I'm also not a sixteen-year-old child."

"Really? Damn, that's just my type."

A moment of horror passes over his face.

"That was a joke!" I reassure him quickly, waving my hands in front of me. "A joke! I promise, I am only into mature, adult men. I'm talking ancient. About as old as your sense of humour."

He bristles, turning back towards the screen. "I thought Nat said you had to make nice with me."

I beam at him. "Oh trust me, I'll break you down one way or another. If you haven't noticed, I can be quite charming. And if that doesn't work, I'll bring in the big guns- Thelma and Louise."

He arches his brow in question.

A grab my chest, one boob in each hand, and I see his eyes widen.

"Thelma," I say, shaking my left hand, "and Louise."

His dark eyes drop to my hands, lingering on the skin under my soft blue tank top, leaving a scorching trail in their path. Something deep in my belly warms at the first sign of Noel being an actual, functioning human being, and not just a meticulously created android. Within the shadows, there's something intense smouldering in those cappuccino eyes.

"Wanna take a picture, it'll last longer," I say with a smirk digging into my cheek, to which he immediately averts his eyes.

"I don't care for what you're implying."

"So you're a boob guy, eh?" I say, delight lacing through my words as I lean in closer to him. "I know, I'm pretty surprised too."

"There's nothing to be surprised about." His lips press into a thin, exasperated line, face returning to its usual stony countenance.

Instantly the charged air evaporates, and he's running his fingers over Cleo again, as if it never happened at all.

I give a shrug. "I just call 'em as I see 'em, Tit Boy."

"Don't call me that," he snaps, a thorny edge to his voice. "Could you leave?"

"Got enough material for your spank bank?"

"I'm going to tell Mark that you're harassing me," he threatens, still refusing to look me in the eye.

I snort. "Tattle-tale."

"Can I spend some time with Cleopatra now? I'm trying to relax. Some of us have jobs, if you hadn't realized," he says, nose tilting upwards and shooting me a sharp, sideways glance.

"Some of us have jobs," I mock him in a bitter soprano, climbing to my feet. There's a subtle complacency written across his face, and I have to patiently remind myself that I am a twenty-four-year-old woman, and not a six-year-old child, and sticking my tongue out is not an appropriate way to communicate with people.

"You do know what a job is, right?" he asks, an infuriating smugness dripping from his tone.

I stick my tongue out at him.

"Cute," he deadpans.

I pivot on my heel, facing into the darkness with knitted brows and a burning irritation in my gut. "I'm bringing out my lowest-cut tops now, Noel. And my best push-up bras. So good job. You've made me do this. You've started a war, and this is your fault."

Then I'm stalking back to my room, arms swinging and lips pouting.

"You're not achieving anything!" he calls out after my retreating figure.

"What was that? Less clothes? Noel, I mean, if you insist!"

Despite the whirlwind of racing thoughts that have set up residence in my mind, when I crawl under my comforter, I finally manage to fall into a light sleep. It isn't until an hour later that a restlessness grips me, and with dreary realization, my parched throat calls for water. Still half-asleep, a river of yawns spilling from my lips, I trek towards the kitchen. My eyes unconsciously drift towards the living room.

The television is still playing, but when I take a curious step inside, Noel's figure is no longer there. I lean over the couch to see him succumbed to sleep, lying peacefully on his side.

Embracing the opportunity, I lean in to get a better look at the tall man. The usual crease in his forehead has softened, along with the tired shadows of his face. His glasses have been left on the ground. He looks younger without them. The frown has disappeared. It's the calmest I've ever seen him, and I can't help the small smile that finds my face.

When I grab a blanket to throw over him, I surrender to the temptation to crouch next to the couch. It's the closest we've ever been, and my eyes sweep over his face, drinking in his sharp jawline and thick, dark lashes. Without the furrowed brows, I can't deny that his face is nice to peek at. Unconsciously, my fingers twitch.

When as I reach out, movement catches the corner of my eye, and I see Cleopatra perched a few feet away. Her green eyes scrutinize me, and I grin, bringing a finger to my lips. As I turn my head, Noel mumbles something in his sleep, and I take it as a sign that I should retreat back to my bed.

"Cleo, this is our little secret, okay?" I wink.

chapter five

CLEO IS TERRIBLE at keeping secrets, apparently.

"So you're into watching people when they sleep now, is it?"

I choke on my wine, palm rushing to cover my mouth as a little red dribbles from the corner. "What?"

"Remember when I told you that Noel's not gonna sue you? Well, if you keep it up, you're gonna have a sexual harassment lawsuit on your hands, and I can't help you."

Despite her words of warning, there's a wicked glint of amusement in Natalya's mint green eyes as she toys with the straw of her Long Island Iced Tea.

I'm still clearing my throat, clutching at my chest as I ignore the looks of concern our waiter is shooting in my direction. Nat takes another sip of her drink, unconcerned with my oncoming death.

"I did not sexually harass him, oh my god. Did he actually say that? Seriously?"

Those narrowed, dark brown eyes flash in my mind

Nat chuckles, nodding, and tucks a golden blonde strand of hair behind her ear. "According to Mark, he insisted you were watching him while he was sleeping. Something about waking up with a blanket and that he wasn't stupid, and that you're a total creep, basically. Keep it up and you can finally cross getting a restraining order off your bucket list."

"That's a stupid thing to have on a bucket list, and I am not getting one."

As my brows drop and lips purse, Nat's dissolving into cheeky laughter once again. It seems her temporary Bridezilla persona has lost to her instinctive obligation to delight in my pain, and I take another spiteful mouth of Merlot. Still, it's one of the rare moments that her shoulders have finally relaxed under her pale blue blouse in months.

And everyone always tries to tell me that day-drinking is irresponsible.

"I wasn't watching him, okay? I put a blanket over him when I got up to get a glass of water because I'm a kind and generous person. I'm practically a saint!" I insist to Nat's unsympathetic grin, and the wine almost jumps passed the rim as I shake my glass for emphasis. "A saint!"

In the back of my mind, I'm reminded of my lingering presence crouched in front of his sleeping figure, along with Cleo's calculated feline glare. But there's no way that he could've known.

Unless Noel's learned the ability to literally talk to his cat. Which, honestly, I can't even say I'd be surprised by.

I mentally curse Cleo. Does sisters before misters mean nothing to her?

"I'm just repeating what Mark told me. I told you to make nice, not get yourself arrested, Vika. Or should I say, arrested again," Nat says, snickering.

"One time! You drunkenly swim around a fountain one time and no one will forget about it! And it was a misdemeanor, come on. You guys never let anything go."

"Well, either way, you better keep your ass out of prison until the wedding because we've already paid for your dinner and of course, for Mark's family, no expense could be spared." She rolls her eyes.

I lean forward with my elbows against the patio table, chin tucked in the heels of my palms."God, I still can't believe you're actually getting married."

The gravity of my words weighs on my shoulders, and I draw a deep breath, nose pinching. I can't ignore how heavy my chest feels.

"Excuse you, I'll have you know many men have tried to take me off the market for years, okay?" she says, brushing her hair over her shoulder. "I'm some premium wife material."

I snort. "I just mean, you're only twenty-five. I love Mark and all, but we're still pretty young, you know? There's so much out there."

I'm called back to high school, giggling with Nat until three in the morning, conceiving one ridiculous fantasy after another about our near adult lives. Somehow broke, unemployed, and essentially homeless never factored into my plan, and yet, here I am, savouring sips from the cheapest wine on the menu and pointedly ignoring all my glaring responsibilities.

A thoughtful expression crosses her face. "Honestly, I never thought I'd get married this early either, but with Mark it just seem s... right. I mean, I can't imagine spending my life with anyone else."

"Fine, Nat! Just rub it in my face! I'll never be enough for you! I get it!"

Nat shoots me a knowing look, flashing the glittering rock on her ring finger with a too-broad grin slapped across her face. "I'm sorry, can you afford this?"

"Ha-ha," I deadpan, fixing her with a half-hearted glare. "I thought I was the escort here, not you."

She laughs and I can't help but join her, always infectious in the way that only hers can be.

Still, Noel's disgruntled brows are burning in the back of my mind. I can't decide if it's my lack of current excitement or just our ridiculous interactions, but I can't stop my thoughts from wandering to the man in the suit. His dark eyes and tousled hair seem to have set up a semi-permanent residency in my head. I reassure myself that his weirdness is completely to blame.

Nat's eyes drift to the watch clutched around her wrist, and I can tell she's gauging how much time she has until she'll really get in trouble for extending her lunch break. "On that subject, have you gotten any interviews? You know that Mark and I are moving into that new place when we come back from our honeymoon, so time's a-ticking, Vika."

I purposely avert my eyes. "That wasn't on the subject at all." I take another gulp of the red wine, and I try to convince myself the pursing of my lips is from the bitter taste, and not because of the way her green eyes are shining with concern.

"Come on, you know you can't live with Mark and I forever. Don't you want your own place? You need to work somewhere, for now at least. To save up."

I lean into my palms as my eyes fall over her shoulder. "I've still got some savings from that shitty telemarketing gig. And, well, I have been working." It doesn't even sound convincing to me.

"Working as in actually receiving paychecks, Vika," Nat says, voice dry, sharp eyes immediately exposing me. "I'm only doing this because I love you, you know? I don't want you to die or something. It worries me, sometimes."

She reaches out and gently touches my wrist, borrowing my gaze.

"I know," I admit, begrudgingly, with a defeated sigh. "I promise, I'll actually put out some resumes and everything tomorrow. Pinky promise."

I hold out my pinky, grinning.

Nat rolls her eyes, hooking her finger with mine, a smile tugging on the corner of her mouth. "Even better, you can promise me that if next week I set you up with an interview, you'll go."

"Interview?" I echo, eyes wide. "Wait, what?"

She beams, nodding and seemingly barely containing herself in her seat. "Mark's cousin owns this breakfast place that's across town-they're looking for a new server. It's a pretty expensive place, so you'll make enough tips to get by, probably. Oh, and I lied and said you had serving experience, but I'm sure you'll be able to bullshit your way through."

The grin that's curved on her face is a touch mischievous and all Natalya. I can only gape as she takes another sip from her iced tea, nonchalance deceived by the bright spark in her eyes.

"What? Where did this come from? Why didn't you start with that?" My jaw hangs open shamelessly.

I pointedly ignore the older ladies at the table next to us that are throwing narrow looks at my outburst. I'm too busy gathering my thoughts to even care. The idea of an actual job seemed so far on the horizon, a career seemingly just an ethereal illusion constructed by everyone around me to be ridiculously rude. Yet here we are.

A coy smirk digs into her cheek as she swirls her straw around her cup. "Well, I wanted to end with good news, so I thought I'd start with getting the whole stalking thing out of the way."

I bristle. "It wasn't stalking."

"Noel feels very different," she sing-songs. "And I suggest you make up with Noel as quick as possible, and I mean it this time, because apparently he loves getting breakfast at this place and I don't think Mark's cousin will be too keen on you assaulting his patrons. Also, he's the Best Man."

I slump in my seat, brows furrowing. "Why does everyone act like I'm the big bad bully and he's some poor little kid that can't defend himself? He can be very mean when he wants to, okay? Why doesn't he have to make nice with me?" I can't help the whine that forms around my words as I fold my arms over my chest.

I willfully ignore how easily Noel, even miles and miles away, reverts me back to a huffy seven-year-old.

"I don't know if you remember, but there was that time you practically slapped a glass at him," she says, pointing her straw at me. "He's still a little bitter over that, apparently."

I roll my eyes. "Oh my god, can no one ever let anything go?"

She grins. "Nope, so next time I'd suggest keeping your hands to yourself, because your job might depend on it."

A concentrated ball of emotion swirls precariously in my chest as we lock eyes. I can feel a prickle at the back of my throat, only further spurred by the soft smile that graces Nat's face, but I swallow it down. The almost tangible reality of an actual job seems to crash into me all at once, and I have to restrain myself from jumping over the table and capturing her in a death hold of a hug.

When the waiter drops the bill on the table, she slaps it at lightning speeds and pulls it towards her. "If you cry, I swear Vika, I'll cancel it right now. Don't do it. I got this one, but next one's on you."

I nod my head, not trusting my words, and down the rest of my drink, allowing the subtle buzz to soothe my nerves.

The ball lingers in my throat all the way home, until I'm in the shower, allowing the water to rinse the day off my skin. In my mind, the sympathy shining in Nat's eyes echoes back to middle school days. Unconsciously, my thoughts travel to my parents.

Despite my keen ability to float unbothered through life, there is still that immigrant parent pressure I can recall being drilled into me since kindergarten- that unachievable expectation to succeed breathing down my neck. Even without their disappointed eyes drilling into the back of my head, the same as when I'd been day drinking behind the bleachers with boys I had no busy being with, the sense still lingers.

I can't help but wonder how different things would've been if they hadn't gotten into that car, a thought that's plagued me ever since it happened. Years and years later, I still can't shake it.

Still, I swallow, collecting myself together again under the showerhead. A job is a job, a step in the right direction, and I focus on that. The flexibility of serving helps, especially with idle thoughts that draw back to the half-written book waiting on my laptop. There's a little bundle of hope beginning in the pit of my stomach.

My shoulders feel a little lighter when I wrap the fluffy white towel around my body. It's a little short. I don't even want to wonder how much Mark paid for smaller towels, but when I check my phone, I see no texts from him, and deem it safe to make a mad-dash for the guest room.

Peeking open the door, silence greets me.

I tip-toe down the hallway with gingerly steps, clutching the towel tight to my body. My door is wide open.

Just as relaxation touches my shoulders, and I loosen my grasp, a voice echoes through the hall.

"Didn't I say to wear more clothes?"

I scream.

And I drop the towel.

chapter six

"HOW THE HELL is dropping your towel your instinctive response in this situation?"

"I flail when I get scared! I'm pretty sure we've already covered this! Don't question my life instincts right now I'm naked!"

"I'm quite aware of both those things," Noel says in a dry voice, neck craned and his framed gaze unwavering from the living room couch.

My face glows as I haphazardly clutch the towel tighter to my body. As soon as I felt the breeze, I'd scrambled to cover up the most important parts, but in vain, only seconds too late for any salvageable dignity.

I try to reassure myself that my near-naked body is barely a blip on his severely low opinion on my existence. Still, I can't help increasingly vulnerable sensation as his dark eyes burn into me.

"Um, you can look away now?"

His eyes narrow. "This isn't your house, if you forgot. I don't know what you're trying to pull here, but I'm not interested."

My lips purse, and I try to tell myself the twisting in my stomach had been there before. "Oh my god, I am not coming on to you. And also- don't act like seeing me naked is the most awful thing in the world, okay? I do squats."

I don't miss the lightning quick flicker of his eyes down the towel, causing an involuntary flush to creep up my neck. His mouth twitches. "This is Mark's house- probably keep the prancing around naked to a minimum. That would be the respectful thing to do."

My teeth grit, and my gaze recalibrates into a glare. "Mark texts me before he comes over so that we avoid awkward situations like this, and also, another key point, he doesn't just materialize out of thin air like a fucking magician. I didn't even hear you come in!"

A severe frown tugs at his mouth. "I'm not a magician."

"Well, your face says otherwise."

I have no idea what that means.

"What does that mean?"

Instead of dignifying his question with an answer I definitely do not have, I grasp the towel tightly to my body and turn on my heel, stalking down the hall. The burning has crawled up to my cheeks now, and I can't handle his scorching, sweeping gaze on my bare skin any longer. When I finally find solace behind a closed door, I sigh.

From my peripherals, I catch my reflection in the full-length mirror propped up against the wall. With a slight frown, I drop the towel, scrutinizing the tanned skin and soft curves that meet my gaze. While I've admittedly missed squat day for some time, it's like Noel's eyes and his words are speaking to me on two different levels. And his coffee dark gaze wandering my skin only further reminds me that the last time I'd had anyone see me naked was Chad and Chad is an entire lifetime ago.

Although I'm not holding my breath for Noel to work out his middle-school feelings to help relieve my sexual frustration, and I'm positive that Nat would actually murder me for even thinking of playing with that kind of fire so close to her wedding.

Which, slightly fair. I clearly did not make the soundest decisions. I slept with and even dated a man named Chad, and despite his magical penis, his name is Chad, and that should be enough.

At least the Bachelor and Chinese food can soothe my involuntarily celibate lifestyle.

With a sigh, I trek over to the drawer and rummage around the mess of wrinkled clothes to find a semi-decent t-shirt and a pair of light grey sweatpants. I figure that the more general blob-like I am, the more I'll appease Noel and succeed in my Maid of Honour mending of unmendable relationships.

Against my better judgement, I trek back into the living room.

He barely acknowledges my presence when I drop down beside him on the couch. I wonder if it's intentional or not, but when he swallows, his Adam's apple dipping in his throat, I know.

"No thank you so much for putting clothes on? Thank you for saving me from the awful tragedy of seeing a naked girl? You are so merciful, oh great Vika?" I snicker as I nudge my elbow towards him.

He fixes me with a measured look. "Do you always take things too far? Is that how you operate?"

"I have no idea what you're talking about." Nat's words swirl in the back of my mind, but despite my former mortification, his frowning presence seems to only brighten the devious grin smeared across my face. "Also, I didn't watch you sleep, by the way. That's a gross exaggeration. I was covering you up with a blanket because I'm a decent person. I know, the concept of decency might be a little new to you."

His eyes are trained on the television screen, nimble fingers lacing through Cleopatra's black and golden fur. "I'd appreciate it if you kept as far away as possible when I'm sleeping."

He replies with a quick glare when I antagonize him with a wiggle of my fingers. "I prefer my men sentient when I kiss them. You'll still be able to wear white on your wedding."

"I'm not dignifying such baseless accusations with a response."

Laughter escapes my lips and I shift closer to him, which he acknowledges with a thin press of his mouth. "While I'd love to go over what a joke is with you, and while it's great that you're watching... what is this? Why are there so many numbers on the screen? No, it's Bachelor time, gimme the remote."

Noel's frown deepens when I lean over him to grab the remote and Cleo deems this a breach of her personal cat bubble, swiftly escaping. The twitch of his jaw tells me that there're more words hovering on the tip of his tongue, but they stay hidden behind his teeth.

"Cleo and I are getting along great, by the way," I reassure him, nodding to her disappearance into the other room. "We're BFFs."

"Cleopatra."

I lean back into the couch cushions, remote in hand. "Hmm?"

"It's Cleopatra, not Cleo. How many times do I have to say that?" There's a hint of resignation in his voice, punctuated by the tired sigh that follows.

I shrug. "It's a nickname. Either that or demon cat, but apparently you have a problem with the last one."

His reply is a deadpan stare, accessorized with his usual deep frown. His body has sunk more into the cushions, shoulders a little less tense as he scratches his stubbled jaw. The masochistic part of me beams at the slightest dip in his hostility.

"Do you think the world would actually go up in flames if you stopped frowning for like, five whole minutes?"

His brows furrow. "I'm not always frowning."

"He says, while frowning."

"Ha-ha," he says dryly, but there's a micro-quirk of his mouth upward. I ignore the way the realization of this sparks down my spine. "The common denominator of my frowns when you're around has a lot more to do with you than with me."

I snort. "And I'm supposed to believe you're just a ball of sunshine the rest of the time? Really? Prancing through meadows?"

"I'm in a better mood when I'm not being forced to watch garbage television." There's a ghost of a smirk on his face.

I gasp, an offended hand coming to press against my chest. "What? How dare you? Attacking the golden standard of prime-time television? You come into my house-"

"Mark's house."

"- and insult my television?"

"Mark's television," he corrects, straight-faced as usual, but when he borrows my gaze, I trick myself that I see a glimmer of amusement.

I don't have any smart comebacks, and so I turn to fish for my cellphone in my pocket. Noel's eyes fall back to the TV despite his mocking comments, and a comfortable silence falls over us. I almost wish I could get photographic evidence for Nat that the two of us could sit next to each other for longer than a minute with no one having a felony hanging over their head.

"All right," I sigh, earning a curious glance from Noel. "I am, once again, extending the olive branch, this time Chinese food included. What do you want? I'm going to order now."

A note of confusion passes over Noel's face. "What?"

I press the numbers in, practically burned into the phone at this point. "I'm buying you Chinese food," I say, a little slower and a little more condescending. "What specifically do you want me to buy for you to eat, Noel?"

Noel's confusion drops for his usual unreadable expression. "I got that. I'm not hungry."

I roll my eyes. "Come on, this is a peace offering. Accept the peace. The peace of food." I punch in the last number, bringing the cellphone to my ear and ushering him to think quicker with my free hand.

If food can't mend our strained relationship, then all hope is lost.

He stumbles slightly. "I don't- I don't know what to get."

I sigh, slightly exasperated as the ringing echoes like a countdown in my ears. "Just get what you usually get, come on, it's ringing, hurry."

Noel's jaw twitches, and when he averts his gaze, he mutters something I can't quite catch. I almost think I see his ears dusting red.

I lean in closer. "What? I didn't catch that. Say it again."

"I don't order my own takeout. Usually someone orders it for me."

Someone says hello on the other end of the receiver, but they are long forgotten.

"What!?"

His alarmed gaze focuses on my cellphone, now clicked off. "Did you just hang up on them?"

He's more concerned with my apparent disrespect than my wide eyes and gaping face, but I find myself more concerned with Noel finally admitting to being an alien from another dimension.

"You've never ordered take out in your life ever?" I ask, a couple decibels above what constitutes an inside voice.

He's refusing to meet my eye, arms folded across his chest. "If I'm late at the office, there's always an assistant around to order something for me, I just eat what's in front of me. I've eaten food in China, I lived in Hong Kong for four years."

"You can't even throw the homeland in my face." My palms drag down the skin of my cheeks. "Ordering your own takeout is part of the entire takeout experience. Oh my god, you don't even have a favorite - do you know what you've even been eating?. What have you been doing all this time? How have you lived such a deprived life?"

His eyes narrow. "Helping run a successful multinational hospitality empire, what about you?"

His bitter dig immediately rolls off my shoulder and I continue to gawk at him as if he's just stepped off of a UFO right in front of me. Which, honestly, might be more believable than what he's saying.

"Yeah, but you haven't even knowingly eaten takeout. All right, okay, so I guess that just means we must get everything," I rationalize, preparing my speech for Nat when she comes over next to find a monumental amount of takeout boxes stuffed in the fridge. "It's just-it has to happen now. That's the only way you can find your one true order."

This is clearly just me being a good person and graciously leading Noel through the gates of take out heaven.

"I said I'm not hungry." His distaste intensifies when he shifts his gaze to see me already on the phone.

"All right, so we'll get an order of spring rolls, the Moo Shu pork, of course, black pepper beef, oh, the Singapore chow mien, and chicken balls are a safe bet, everyone loves chicken balls, so definitely an order of chicken balls. Are you getting this? Yes, there's more, one sec, I have your menu around here somewhere..."

chapter seven

AFTER THE ORDER is placed, despite all of Noel's weak protests, I'm grinning.

He's practically folded into himself, the exasperation on his face growing stronger the longer I look at him. It's been a couple minutes of this. Him obviously avoiding my stare, and of me obviously staring. There's this bizarre cognitive dissonance in his six-year-old temper tantrum and the sleek, black tie loose around his neck, and I can't help but laugh.

"Why are you laughing?" he asks, eyes fixated on the screen.

"Why do you always hang around here if you hate it so much?" I counter. Despite the mocking undertones, I can't help the curiosity itching under my words.

He's more questions than answers, despite the fact that I'm clearly a joy to be around, but whatever.

His expression softens just a smidgen. "Because Cleopatra's here."

I tilt my head, and something inside of me warms at the change. "Yeah, but why don't you take her home? Instead of barging in here at all hours of the night. Unless, seeing me naked was your plan the entire time!"

When his gaze slides over to meet mine, narrowed and unimpressed, I'm beaming.

"It's complicated," he admits with a sigh, threading a hand through his dark hair. "Cleopatra has to stay here. That's the way things have to be for now."

The insatiable curiosity that always seems to get me into more trouble than I can get out of wants me to press him further, and for a moment I open my mouth to ask more, but then it's shut again. His closed-off expression tells me it's the end of that conversation, and for some inexplicable reason, I don't want him to leave just yet.

I reassure myself it's only because he needs to be introduced into the wonderful world of Moo Shu pork. And not because I keep wondering how soft his hair really is.

"Mysterious. If you were trying not to turn me on, try harder."

He opens his mouth to rebuke, a telling pinch of his brows, but I cut him off with a swift lift to my feet.

"All right, I'm putting you on Bachelor duty. I expect a full report when I come back. I'm serious here." I hold a threatening finger to further my point. "The importance is in the details."

He bristles. "I'm not watching your garbage show or eating your garbage food."

I shoot him a cheeky grin, grabbing my jacket from the chair I'd left it crumpled up on. "Keep an eye on Katrina, she's the crier."

As the door almost closes shut, I hear Noel mutter some sort of response under his breath. A soft smile involuntarily curves on my face. A part of me realizes that I'm probably going to be scolded later for teasing him so much, and I have absolute faith this will get back to Natalya, but there's a little bounce in my too-quick steps back home, and I'm not entirely sure it's because of the food I'm carrying.

Although the food does help. My wallet is crying a little bit- a lot a bit honestly, but I reassure myself that I'm being a good person, and therefore it's justified. I'm not doing this for myself, I'm doing this for Noel.

So it's okay.

And the extra wontons are also justified because they're extra wontons. They're always justified. Because they're wontons.

A laugh that sounds suspiciously like a cackle escapes my lips when I step through the door, plastic bags brimming with a plethora of noodle-meat combinations in hand, and Noel's eyes widen to saucers.

"Are you ready for your mind to be blown?" A devious grin spreads across my face.

"You do realize that there's only two of us. And that I'm not hungry. So really, that's all for you." He looks seriously concerned. "You're going to die."

My grin never falters as I dump myself next to him on the couch and drop the straining plastic bags onto the steel and glass coffee table. The delicious aroma has been teasing me the entire walk home, and my stomach growls as I begin not-so carefully hauling the boxes from the bag.

There's no time for grace when there's take out.

"Updates."

"What?"

"Updates," I repeat, nodding to the TV, grabbing the aluminum containers. "I asked for details."

There's a beat of silence, and I'm expecting another crass comment about my apparent garbage taste in television when I glance up at him, but all I get is a sigh.

"The girls all got upset because that one blonde woman apparently stole him away from the group date, which is ridiculous, they're on a competitive dating show. Then he had some rehearsed television moment with Meghan. Also, Katrina cried," he mumbles, albeit a tad begrudgingly, eyes refusing to stray from the screen.

A colossal smile lights up my face. "Wow, is Monday going to be our Bachelor date night now?"

"Let's not get too ahead of ourselves."

I laugh, opening up the last aluminum container and releasing a delicious waft of pork goodness into the air. I can feel myself salivate. "All right," I say, rubbing my hands together with wide, excited eyes. "What do you want to start with?"

"I said I'm not hungry." His cool exterior is as thick as ever.

"Come on," I whine, pouting slightly. "Just try it, is all I ask. Pick something, whatever you want. Let me show you the way of my people."

He arches a brow.

"It would be rude of you to refuse. Come on, rich boy," I say, scooping up a delicious helping of Moo Shu pork on my chopsticks and slowly meandering it through the air, closer to his mouth.

Noel pulls back, a disturbed mark on his face. "Aren't you going to get some dishes?"

I shoot him a look. "Dude, they already come in dishes. That's what the containers are for. Why would I make more work for myself when the ways of Bamboo Buddha China House have already fixed this problem for me? That's why there's literally no downside to take out."

"Except increasing your risk of colorectal cancer."

I beam. "That's half the fun!"

My answer doesn't seem to reassure his doubts at all as he continues to shoot me a wary stare, mouth pressed together and uninviting of the pork noodle I've got compiled on my chopsticks.

And I don't even know how, at this point, because I'm two seconds away of going straight up Neanderthal on everything in front of me.

When I hum and bring it closer, he turns his head like a toddler. The added airplane noises also produce similar results. Trains aren't any more tempting. My shoulders slump, a little defeated when the car yields absolutely nothing.

"Noel! Try it!"

"I'm not hungry."

"One bite! Don't be a baby!"

"Don't call me a baby. And still no. Stop with the train. Don't choo-choo at me. No. I refuse."

My eyes sharpen. "Don't make me get physical."

"Don't touch me." He returns my challenging stare

A small noise of surprise erupts from Noel as I lunge for him with one hand, pushing him down, the other still tightly grasping the chopsticks. It's one of the only talents I can speak of, the maternal genetics channelling all the ancestry I have, but it's coming in handy. He's caught off guard by my sudden attack, and so goes down easily with wide eyes and flailing limbs.

Taking advantage of his weakened state, I jump into his lap to pin him down, earning another guttural sound of concern. His glasses are slightly off-kilter. A smirk carves into my face.

I dangle the noodles above him. "Say ah!"

"Get off me," he mumbles, turning his head and fixing his glasses. "I'm telling Mark."

"I'm telling Mark," I mimic him in a mocking falsetto. "Come on little boy, eat the Moo Shu pork and I promise I won't touch you for the rest of the night."

His jaw flexes, arms still somehow crossed over his chest. "I'm not a little boy. And don't mock me, what are you, a fifth-grader?"

I grin, pulling my elbows closer together, shimmying closer to him. "Do these look like they belong to a fifth-grader?"

Something deep in my belly tightens when Noel's eyes not so inconspicuously drift down to the dip in my v-neck, and it appears he's barely recognized the action himself until it's too late, his eyes are snapping back to mine. I laugh, dangling the noodles closer to his mouth.

"If you eat the tasty noodles, maybe I'll even give you a reward."

He turns his head. "Get off me, I'm serious."

There's a beat of quiet, both of us stubbornly refusing to budge from our positions, and then a sigh spills from my lips. I pout and my shoulders fall slightly.

"Please? Just try it. And I promise I'll leave you alone for the rest of the night. I'll even brush Cleo."

There's a pause. "Cleopatra."

"I will brush Cleopatra."

There's another moment, and then, slowly, he turns his head back towards me. For a moment I'm shocked, when he ever so slightly parts his lips open, pointedly staring in the other direction.

"Ah," he deadpans.

With a wide grin, too-pleased than I honestly should be with myself, I drop the noodles into his mouth. Then he's thoughtfully chewing, still refusing to meet my eye.

"And?" I prompt, leaning in. "The verdict?"

He swallows, and when his eyes lock with mine, a shiver crawls down my spine. I'm suddenly more aware of the position we're in, with Noel's back pressing into the couch and my body hovering over him, unconsciously leaned in more than I'd expected.

His dark eyes are burning into me, and they're closer than I've ever seen them, magnified even further by his glasses. There's flecks of green and light brown, swirling with something I can't quite pin-point, and I swallow.

"It's... good." Noel meets my gaze.

I nod, slowly. "That's... good."

There's quiet, and I'm expecting him to roll his eyes, shove me off, do something, anything, but he doesn't. He does nothing, and I'm frozen, unable to do anything either.

He parts his lips to say something, and there's a sharp intake of breath at the back of my throat.

"Guys?"

My eyes widen and immediately I shoot up, arms flailing and heartbeat thudding in my ears. My reliable lack of hand-eye coordination has me tumbling off the side of the couch and catching the edge of the coffee table on the side of my head, a piercing pain blossoming on my scalp.

"Um, hey Mark," Noel says while fixing his glasses, but his voice sounds a fraction off, and his eyes widen when then land on me. "Christ, are you okay?"

"I'm fine!" I blurt out, voice a few octaves higher than usual, protectively rubbing my head with a wince. My cheeks burn. "I'm totally okay! It's, uh, hey Mark!"

Mark appears, a boyish grin gracing his face, and a pizza box in his hand. I'm still a little disoriented, a ball tight in the pit of my stomach, but his face doesn't appear suspicious, which is a good sign.

My pulse is still thudding in my ears.

"Hey guys, what're you up to? I thought I'd bring pizza- I texted you, but I guess you didn't get it."

I suck my teeth. "I was just- Chinese food. I was making him try Chinese food. That's all that was happening." Despite the fact that I'm trying to sound as normal as possible, even I can hear the slight upticks of panic in my voice.

"She forced me," Noel agrees, a little too quickly, and I shoot him a glare.

Mark shrugs, not the least bit suspicious. "Guess we'll be eating pretty well tonight."

"Cool!" I chirp, maybe a little too eager. "I forgot something in my room, so I'm going to go grab that!"

I can't meet Noel's gaze as I jump to my feet and smooth down my hair. Despite the lack of questions from Mark, I still don't feel entirely comfortable, especially because I don't even know if I can explain what happened to myself.

Mostly because there would be nothing to explain, because nothing happened.

My lack of sexual contact in more time than I'd like to admit is tricking my mind, I reassure myself while bolting towards my room. I'm sure Noel's feelings for me don't fall outside the circle of annoyed, irritated, or exasperated.

I just need to get laid.

Like, yesterday.

As I push my door open, I stifle a laugh when I hear Noel's voice.

"Hey Mark, do you think I look like a magician?"

chapter eight

"AS A STRONG, independent female in the 21st century, what do you do when you're feeling... sexually frustrated?"

I steal another sip of my cheap, dry wine, tilting my head as I wait for a response. The kitchen tile is cool against my bare thighs, and the floor-to-ceiling windows reveal the blushing notes of twilight outside. There's a warmth buzzing underneath my skin.

The cat, like always, does not respond.

I sigh. "Cleo, I'm gonna be real with you- straight woman to cat here. I need to get laid. Like, yesterday."

Cleo continues to stare, perched on the counter across from me, green eyes piercing into my soul. I feel weirdly comforted by her feline presence, even with her usual look of contempt.

"I hear you, definitely, I should go out. I'm not going to find any solutions to my getting laid problem alone in here, but I'm lazy. I don't want to try. I want something easy. I want... oh man, I'm gonna end up calling Chad tonight aren't I?"

Cleo licks at her paw.

My shoulders slump. "I know, I know- Cleo, I hear you. Chad is... Chad's a bad idea. Yes, his penis is magical. But also, he hates to cuddle. And you know, Cleo, I love to cuddle. So it's definitely a terrible idea," I say, taking another generous sip. "I definitely should not call Chad, no matter what happens."

When Cleo pauses her licking for a moment, wide emerald eyes shifting to me, I take this as a quiet agreement. It sounds like a better idea the more that I say it out loud- remind myself of why he's my ex-boyfriend in the first place.

My thoughts betray me as they wander to thick black frames and coffee dark eyes, but no, I tell myself, that's an even worse idea than Chad. At least I know that Chad sees me as a human being, one he would also like to have sex with, and not some loud, greedy gremlin.

Involuntarily, that hooded gaze from the Chinese food episode flickers in my memory- the incident that apparently ignited this insatiable need inside of me, but even then, it's quickly followed by the ghost of Nat's scolding voice.

Nope- that's not even an option. The options are sleep with Chad, or not sleep with Chad. And the only actual decision should be not sleep with Chad, and continue having one-sided conversation with the most unimpressed cat in the world while drowning myself in cheap box wine.

I hadn't even seen Noel in the last week, and I can't quiet the thought that he's avoiding me. Not that I'd particularly noticed or whatever.

Still, when I heave another sigh, I can feel my resolve crumbling. My phone lays next to me, open on a new text message, with Chad's name written on the top. It's just sex, a traitorous little voice in the back of my head murmurs. It means nothing.

I pout. "Cleo, what do I do?"

"Stop talking to the cat, for one."

I jump at the new presence, staring up with wide eyes to see Nat grinning in the doorway. Her eyebrows are raised, a condescending glimmer in her gaze as she looks from me to the cat.

My brows furrow. "Excuse you, Cleo and I are having a private conversation."

Nat laughs, padding over to where I'm sitting on the floor and wiggling her fingers down to me. "Come on, up, up, let's get you dressed and out of here. The cat might not be able to help you get laid, but I might."

"Nat! You're a taken woman now!" I allow her to pull me up from my sad little spot on the kitchen tile. "You can't throw out propositions like that anymore!"

She rolls her eyes. "Come on," she says, stealing the plastic cup from me- a substitute for Mark's wine glasses that I trusted myself not at all with. "We'll get some lipstick on you and we'll go out. You're either getting laid or getting drunk and none of those are particularly awful, are they?"

I shrug, a small smile finding my face as Nat's gentle grip pulls me into the bathroom. The more distractions the better, and I allow one last fleeting glance at my phone abandoned on the kitchen floor. A sign, I tell myself. A sign that crawling back to Chad again will not tonight's conclusion.

But as the night grows older and my reality grows fuzzy, the getting laid part of her offer seems less and less likely. No one particularly piques my interest, and despite a few bedroom eyes and nauseating pick up lines, the only thing I'll be hugging by the night's end is either Nat, but she's got Mark, or more likely my oversized bottle of wine.

Maybe Cleo will finally warm up to me in my time of need. Weren't cats able to pick up on this type of thing?

Despite the refreshing distraction that Nat offers, when we're both stumbling back to Mark's place, all wobbly knees and boisterous laughter, there's still an unfulfilled need humming underneath my skin. And my thoughts keep drifting to Chad's number burned in my memory, a promise, if anything, for a good time. A bonus, too, if I could fuck whatever this is out of my system and stop holding loose associations of it with someone who it had no business being associated with.

I was doing this for the good of Nat's wedding. She should thank me for getting laid.

As we finally reach Mark's door, Nat murmurs something about taking a call, and I don't even have to look at her phone to know who's on the other end. Instead, I roll my eyes, tell her to pass on a hello from me to Mark, and desert her in the hallway.

Because the only thing that's specifically calling for me is my bed, it seems.

As soon as I step inside, I surrender to Mark's soft beige sectional. A groan crawls up my throat, frustration of the not sexual and definitely sexual kind brewing stronger inside me.

Somehow I always forget that excessive drinking only makes the whole dying-alone-forever thing worse.

My eyes drift to the purse I'd dumped haphazardly on the floor next to me. The purse with my phone. The phone with Chad's number. The number that will get me laid tonight.

I pause, but as the memories of a certain pair of dark brown eyes flood into my mind, further inspiring the dizziness that's clawing into my consciousness, I rifle through my purse with purpose. I am, after all, a weak creature. And the longer I steep in the almosts and what ifs, the what could've beens, the more my resolve begins to dissolve.

"Vika?"

Just as my fingers curl around my cell phone, I look up.

There's Noel, standing in the hallway, head tilted to the side ever so slightly. He's not wearing his glasses for the first time. Cleo's bundled up in his arms, looking the most at peace I've ever seen.

Noel's face possesses the usual shadows from lack of sleep, but his brown eyes are lit up in surprise. He's wearing a black dress shirt with the sleeves rolled up, or as I like to call, my kryptonite

"Are you spending your Friday night hanging out with your cat?"

He blinks, brows furrowing softly, and my answer is written all over his face. The worst part is for some reason, the alcohol humming under my skin reads this as endearing. Were his eyelashes always this long?

Goddamnit.

I drop my phone, and there's a beat of quiet between us. My eyes shift to the door, where Nat is on the other side, but then they shift back to Noel and fuck it. Liquid courage is whispering all the wrong-but-so-right things to me.

Noel watches with curious eyes as I climb up and stumble my way over to him, a fierce determination burning in my chest. Any reasonable thoughts that live inside me have already fallen asleep hours ago.

"What are you doing?" Noel asks, voice softer than usual.

At my oncoming presence, Cleo jumps out of his arms and honestly that's fine with me. The fewer obstacles between Noel and I the better, according to the pleased thrumming in the pit of my stomach. I admit that I'm done questioning the very questionable reactions I have when he's around.

Noel's entire body tightens when I reach out and gently grip his chin, a thoughtful hum in the back of my throat. "You'll do."

His Adam's apple dips in his throat. "What?"

Despite his frozen muscles, he offers little resistance when I turn his head, my eyes dragging appreciatively along the sharp contours of his face. The usual five o'clock shadow dusting his skin is darker than usual, in a way that I'm not complaining about at all.

"I never really knew that I had a thing for jawlines until I met you. You have a really nice jaw; you know that? It could win awards, if there were awards for jaws. The jaw Oscars. The jawscars. You'd win. I'd bet on it."

Maybe I should've stopped at seven tequila shots.

He blinks again, absolute bewilderment reflected in his eyes. "Thank you? That doesn't explain- what are you doing?"

His voice grows rougher as my fingertips trail down the hollow of his throat, steadily committing the feel of his skin to memory. I smile when he swallows, breathing shallow, pinned underneath my gaze.

My soft smile translates into a smirk when my wandering hands continues their path downward, to which he unfortunately captures my wrist two seconds before impact.

"Christ! You can't try and grab people!"

I meet his gaze with a cheeky grin. "Hmm, I wonder if you're like a shiny ken doll down there."

His stare hardens as he gently but firmly moves my offending hands away. "Vika, what are you actually doing right now? Are you drunk?"

Despite the hard line of his mouth, the depths of his pupils draw me closer. The ghost of his touch still burns against my wrist, there's an unmistakable heat radiating from his body, the reminder travelling deliciously down to the base of my spine.

"I'm sorry," I say, looking up at him through my lashes, not very sorry at all. "How unchivalrous of me. Has anyone every told you that you have beautiful eyes? Also, can I kiss you?"

"What? I-'

I arch a brow, his mouth just heartbeats away from mine. "Is that a no?"

He swallows. "Well, no, I mean-"

"Good."

I'm sealing my mouth against his, weaving my fingers through his hair and fiercely tugging him closer. Under my touch, I feel him immediately freeze. The realization that I have crossed every single boundary that's ever existed dawns on me, and despite all my instincts, I begrudgingly pull away. My palms drop to rest on the nape of his neck, and I meet his eyes. They're wide, searching, as they linger over my face.

As I part my lips to apologize, beg him not to say anything to Mark, blame the too-many tequila shots coursing through my veins, he ducks his head. And then, he's kissing me back. Mouth moving against mine, hands curled on my hips, torso flush against my own.

And it's good.

Actually, it's fucking fantastic. In moments he's tilting his head and deepening the kiss, licking into my mouth, hot and wet and hard in all the best ways. The need burning inside me is reflected in the way Noel drags me closer, fingertips just as greedy to cover as much skin as possible.

His touch is digging the perfect pressure into my hipbones, and I'm reaching an entirely new level of dizzy, drunk on his breath melting on my tongue. I can't even question his ridiculously apt technique before he's tugging on my bottom lip with his teeth, causing me to arch my back into him, desperate.

I honestly didn't have any sort of actual plan when I'd jumped him, but all my expectations immediately dissolve between his lips.

I would almost be embarrassed if I wasn't more concerned with the delirious need to get closer, too far gone to even question the logistics of what the hell is going on. Instead, I'm drinking in the little hum in the back of his throat, spurred when I grind my hips shamelessly into his, and smirking when I plainly feel that no, he's definitely not a ken doll down there. I can't help but be mindlessly ecstatic that he's feeling it as much as I am.

The only thing I can concentrate on is his mouth on mine and the simultaneously irritating and delicious friction of our clothes between us.

So much so, in fact, that I'm only mildly annoyed when Noel pauses, and still thoughtlessly trying to kiss him when the reverberating of a door slam pierces my thoughts.

I jump back, panting, as if his skin has literally burned me.

"Vika! I'm here on Chad patrol! You're in lockdown all night! Drunk Vika is too horny for her own good! Where are you?"

With the new distance, I'm able to get a better look at Noel. His dark hair is mussed, a consequence of my wandering hands, and his pupils are blown, wide and dark, focused on me. His bottom lip is wet and kiss bitten. Echoes of me are written all over him, and I'm not sure if it's Nat or Noel who's causing my pulse to trip.

Our gazes ignite in the air, and I swallow.

I bring a finger to my lips, and he nods.

Then I jump out from behind the wall, grinning too broadly at Nat, hooking my hands behind me in innocence. "You've come to seduce me, have you?"

She throws her head back and laughs, completely oblivious to the fact that Noel, just out of sight, is haphazardly fixing his wrinkled shirt. I absently pat my hair down, hoping it's slightly less chaotic and obvious than his. My heartbeat continues to thud too hard in my chest.

"Excuse you, I'm a taken woman, but I did order pizza, so that'll do," she says, shrugging off her jacket.

"Boo," I tease, sticking my tongue out.

Noel seizes this opportunity to disappear into Mark's room, and takes the whirlwind of confusing thoughts with him. There are still lingering traces of his presence all of my skin, my drunken determination still trying to piece together the surreal of it all. A part of me recognizes that my stupidity could have monumentally fucked everything up, from not only our strange relationship but more importantly Nat's wedding, or as she likes to point out, currently her entire life.

But there's another part of me that really wants to do it again.

chapter nine

I'M LATE.

Which isn't anything terribly new, honestly, but in this case it is just terrible. Because I'm late for something actually important, which is essentially the rest of my life, and as someone who rather enjoys partaking in the general human experience, being late is crushing any and every hope for the rest of my life not being homeless, starving, and cold in an alleyway. And that's not good.

I'm wearing my smartest blazer, hair pulled back in a way that says I'm not doing this because I forgot to take a shower but because of efficiency, and a pair of plain black flats I'd stolen from Nat's closet.

I even shoved a muffin in my face as some excuse of breakfast before I'd dashed out the door.

I've determined that the people who eat breakfast are the people who have any semblance of their life together, and damn it, I'm going to be one of them, even if for show.

Except now, I probably won't, because I am very, very late.

I'm haphazardly weaving through the crowds of people ambling down the sidewalk, my steps are a beat too quick and slightly off kilter. The leather folder clutched in my sweaty palm has my poor excuse of a resume pressed neatly inside, and I keep running my tongue over my teeth, unable to escape the nagging thought that there's a lipstick smudge, even after the thirtieth time.

My eyes dart down to my phone again, and as another minute ticks by I feel another morsel of my soul die.

Although, really, it's just less for Nat to kill when she finds out I completely bombed the interview she set up by being dreadfully, appallingly late and she slashes me into itty bitty pieces with a machete.

As the sign Viva La Breakfast comes into view, my heartbeat picks up pace to follow suit with my legs, and then I'm bursting through the doors with a small gasp and a river of I'm sorry's.

Then, as if no time has passed at all, I'm shaking this tall man's hand, mouth stretched in what I hope is a bright, employable smile, and thanking him for his time, really, so much, looking forward to hearing from him, honestly, truly, thank you so much for the opportunity.

As I push open the door from the back office, with a white-knuckled grip still on my resume, I can barely remember what happened. My weak sense of logic reassures me I clearly had some sort of interaction, since it's hour an hour later, but all I can focus on is how dry my mouth feels.

Just as I'm heading out and seriously considering throwing myself into traffic, a familiar head of dark hair catches my eye, and I pause.

Tucked in the corner booth is Noel. His thick frames are settled on the bridge of his nose, a coffee hovering underneath his lips and an honest to god newspaper spread out in front of him. I can see his eyes scanning down the page, and it's the first time I've seen him since he'd been dragging my bottom lip into his mouth.

There's a split-second where I see myself stepping out onto the street, climbing onto a bus and going home to bury myself within the sanctuary under my covers, but then my feet pivot.

I drop in the seat opposite to Noel, grinning brightly at him as my leather folder smacks hard against the wooden tabletop.

"Fancy meeting you here."

His head shoots up, eyes wide and swimming with bewilderment. There's a beat where his eyebrows furrow as if he's trying to decipher if I'm a sleep-deprived figment of his imagination or not. I grin brighter.

"Are you stalking me?"

I snort, curving my fingers around his porcelain cup and pulling it towards me. "No," I say, before finishing his coffee in one swift gulp. "And that isn't a very nice thing to ask someone who went through the worst interview in the existence of the entire universe. I'm sensitive right now. Also, was that decaf?"

"Interview?" His mouth twitches. "And no, but it was mine."

I roll my eyes. "I checked their menu last night- with the prices they think are reasonable, I hope you get free refills. And I would make a joke that if I wanted to work here I'd better improve my happy endings, judging by how much an eggs benedict costs, but that would require me to actually get the job and that's pretty unlikely at this point."

"Did it go that bad?" he asks, tilting his head.

A bitter laugh escapes my lips. "Bad? More like catastrophic. I was ten minutes late and I barely remember what I even said. There's a real possibility that I just sat there and drooled. Maybe I went into excruciating detail of my childhood trauma with rabbits. Who knows?"

"Rabbits?"

I half-heartedly wave my hand. "It's a long story. Essentially they're demon creatures and Watership Down is not a children's movie."

He pauses, but doesn't press it any further. A frown weighs down his mouth when he reaches for his coffee cup, only to remember that it's empty. I choke back a laugh.

"Anyway," he says, shooting me a sharp look. "Why were you late?"

At the quick reminder of my terrible fate, I sigh, shoulders slumping. "Writing. It doesn't really make sense to other people, but sometimes I get in these weird writing frenzies. They're almost out of my control."

Out of habit, I pause to check if he's still listening, expecting that glazed film over his eyes that's inevitable whenever writing speak leaves my mouth. Instead, his elbows are propped on the table, chin resting on his entwined fingers, and he nods for me to continue. Involuntarily, something inside of me warms.

"The only problem with these weird grooves is that they usually happen at night," I continue, "And I have the shitty habit of ignoring multiple alarm clocks if I don't get enough sleep." I heave another sigh, sleep still heavy on my lashes. "My body is actively working against me. It sucks."

What I purposely omit is the fact that the writing hysteria that I'd surrendered to was definitely inspired by the unrelieved tension buzzing under my skin from the ghost of his fingertips singeing into my hips.

It didn't help that his unusual lack of presence had only further ignited this fire, and rather than actually confronting any of the total fuckery I had brought onto myself, fictional characters I had ultimate control over served as the greatest of distractions.

There's still a hint of unease lingering in the back of my throat, though, reflected in the way I can see his shoulders tighten.

"Christian is a charitable guy. I'm sure you'll be fine." Something like a smile tugs at the corner of his lips.

A silence settles in the air, just a touch enough uncomfortable that I shift in my seat. His eyes are fixed on the newspaper again. I draw a deep breath.

"What are you doing right now? Let's go somewhere. If I'm not distracted than I'm going to freak myself out over nothing with this interview. And that's going to be awful," I say, ignoring the tinge of nerves that are collecting in the pit of my stomach and covering it up with a smile.

His mouth presses into a thin line, a pained look crossing his face. "Vika, I don't-"

"Oh, come on," I groan. "Don't be like that, don't be weird. I get it, but come on. We kissed. It's whatever. The world isn't ending."

He swallows, and there's some sort of emotion conflicted in his dark eyes. "I know, but we... we shouldn't have done it."

My brow quirks. "But we did."

"But we shouldn't have."

"But Noel, we so did."

"Aren't you worried about the consequences?" he asks, a crease etched in his forehead.

I shrug. "What? We actually get along for Nat and Mark's wedding? The horror."

He seems to consider what I say, but the apprehension is still fresh on his face. It doesn't really make sense that he's the same man who had me gasping for breath underneath him.

His lips part as if he's about to say something, but I cut him off.

"Alright Noel, yes, we shouldn't have done it, but bottom line here. Do you regret it?"

There's a long pause. I ignore the twisting in my stomach.

He sighs. "No."

My shoulders instantly relax, and I can feel the tension unraveling from inside of me as I meet his gaze, the edge of his mouth barely curling up.

"Then it's fine. Let's move on. You can distract me from the catastrophe that is currently my life. Maybe if you come, you might actually have what us poor people call fun. You do know what that is, right?"

He throws me a dry look. "I am aware of what fun is."

"Great!" I beam, clapping my hands. "Let's go! If we don't leave in the next thirty seconds, I might spontaneously combust, so let's get a move on."

Noel sighs, eyes shifting to the gold watch clutched to his wrist. "I actually have a meeting soon, I only came for a quick breakfast..."

I groan, melodramatically throwing up my arms. "Oh, come on, what time's your meeting, Mr. Important Business Man?"

"Eleven."

My face drops. "Are you serious? That's like three hours away. No, nope, I refuse to hear anymore lame excuses. We're getting out of here. Up, up, up," I usher him, waving my hands as I slide out of the seat, grabbing my leather folder.

There's a moment of conflict, eyes dragging from me to the newspaper. Then a defeated sigh spills from his lips as he's throwing a few bills on the table and peeling himself off of the leather seat. A grin stretches across my face.

"I really can't be late for this meeting," he murmurs, but still obediently follows me out of the restaurant.

I roll my eyes. "I'm sure the Queen of England can wait."

"You do know that I work in the hotel business, right?" he asks, falling into step with me on the sidewalk.

"I actually do not care. No job talk. We're supposed to be distracting here. All job talk is officially off the table. Now this might be tough, but do you actually do anything other than work? These are what we call 'interests' or 'hobbies'."

He shoots me a deadpan stare. "People with money have interests and hobbies."

"Oh, no, here I was trying to bridge the alien-human dichotomy," I say, a shit-eating grin finding my face. Noel is even more unimpressed.

The few stray rays of sunshine peaking through the clouds warm my skin, and the slightest breeze tousles the ends of Noel's dark hair. The twisting and turning in my stomach that had accompanied all thoughts of Noel has finally disentangled, and there's a bizarre touch of relaxation to my shoulders while walking beside him. Faint memories of the area are directing me towards the quaint little park that's only a couple of blocks ahead, with Noel apparently trusting me to guide the way.

When I peek over, he's got his hands stuffed into the pockets of his pants, eyes set forward. I smile.

"You know you're safe to come back to the apartment, right? I'm not gonna jump you if I get you in an enclosed space. Although, I'm surprised you lasted as long as you did without Cleo in your life. I think she misses you," I tell him, playfully bumping my shoulder into his. "She even almost let me touch her the other day."

"Cleopatra," he says without missing a beat. "And I wasn't... avoiding you."

I hum. "What do you call actively keeping away from someone for long periods of time?"

"I was busy," he insists, pointedly avoiding my stare. "My job is quite demanding."

I scoff, a smirk digging into my cheek. "Right, sure. Too busy for me? I'd believe. Too busy for Cleo? Yeah, right. You have an unhealthy attachment to that cat. And I say that in a it's kind of adorable way."

There's a moment of quiet, and I turn to see him aggressively staring at the ground, a hint of pink dusting the tips of his ears. I ignore the impulse to press him further, colour the blush darker.

Nat murdering me seems inevitable. Now it's a toss up of quick and painless, or tortuously slow, and I'd like to keep the former as an option.

"Where are we going?" he mumbles, still averting his gaze.

"The park," I announce, gesturing broadly as we come up the winding gravel path, bordered by wide, expansive maple trees and bright bursts of dandelions. "Beautiful, relaxing, and most importantly free."

Noel pauses, hovering on the sidewalk with a wary crease in his brow. His lips press in a thin, thoughtful line. I frown at his hesitation.

"You alright there, man?" I ask, curious as I lean close to him, hands linked behind my back.

He blinks, and then shakes his head, taking off without me. "I'm fine. Hurry up, I don't have all day."

Despite his abrasive tone, I'm less than deterred as I follow after him. His strides are long, essentially doubling mine, and his chin is lifted with the sort of posture none of my teachers could ever nag into me. Still, I let my eyes drag appreciatively down the expanse of his back to just under his spine, a smirk carving onto my face.

He throws a look over his shoulder. "You coming?"

I nod, throwing him a broad grin and a salute. "Sir, yes, sir!"

It only takes a few quick strides to catch up to him, and then we're both falling in step once again, the gravel crunching underneath our shoes. His dark eyes are roaming from the infinite blue sky to the budding green leaves, never lingering for too long on any one thing. Despite the faint chirps of sparrows, his brows are still furrowed.

"Are you scanning for any hobos? Scared one might touch you or something? Because this is actually a nice park, okay. I didn't take you to some sketchy underpass or anything," I reassure him, leaning my head forward to gauge his troubled face.

He catches my gaze, dry as usual, and his mouth twitches. "I know. I've been here before."

"What? Really?" I instantly perk up, brows jumping up my forehead in shock. "No way."

His shoulders drop, but his hands remain snug in his pockets, gaze trailing over past the trees to one of the tall, looming buildings a few streets away. "There's a Carlton hotel, if you haven't noticed."

"Huh, cool. So when you're too stressed out do you get some poor assistant to walk around here and report back to you how it was?"

"No," he says, deadpan. "I used to come here with my dad, is all. When I was a child."

I don't miss the way he swallows, Adam's apple dipping precariously in his throat. There's a softness to his voice that I've never heard from him before and for some reason it's still echoing in my mind, like I can't let it go just yet.

I grin. "Are we unlocking Noel Carlton backstory right now?"

"No, you are not."

"Have I finally broken you down?" I continue, ignoring him. "Is this like level five or something? Have I actually done it?" I press a shocked hand against my chest.

He only rolls his eyes in response.

Still, I can't ignore the warmth that's building at the bottom of my spine as I steal another glance at his face, studying the careful way the resident notch in his brows has softened.

"What?" he snaps, after a moment of silence that I hadn't quite acknowledged yet. "I was a child once, yes, I know. It's impossible for you to imagine. I'm a robot. I get it."

My gaze of wonder breaks with a laugh, and I shake my head. "No!" I protest, but the look he fixes me with is doubtful. "Seriously! I was thinking of how cute you would be. But also, now I'm thinking of a kid that hates everything as much as you do, and actually, it's hilarious."

He bristles. "I don't hate everything."

"Yes, yes, my bad. Everything but your cat. My mistake."

He opens his mouth to make a rebuttal, but he's interrupted by a shrill ringing from his pocket, and he pauses. I stop too, a little disappointed that his argument dies on his tongue as he brings the phone to his ear, turning his back towards me. Something inside of me twists as he murmurs words I can't quite make sense of.

When he hangs up and turns back towards me, mouth open and ready to pour out some excuse, a rueful smile tugs on my lips. "Go Mr. Important Business Man, I'll be fine."

He ducks his head slightly, clearing his throat. "Yeah, sorry," he says, voice a little rougher than usual. "Work."

There's a moment where we're both unsure of what to do with our bodies, the air saturated with an uncomfortable tinge that has both of us go to make some sort of movement but then think better immediately after. Our eyes meet.

"I'll see you later," I promise him, giving him a small wave and clutching my leather folder to my chest.

He nods, fixing his glasses, and then turns on his heel without another word. I watch with bated breath as he disappears down the gravel path and out of my sight, leaving me alone underneath the maple trees.

This cannot be a healthy development, and I do not have enough money for a therapist that doesn't feed me drinks or sleep on a cardboard box.

chapter ten

"YEAH YOU LIKE THAT? Does this turn you on?" I spit, nose pinched and eyes narrowed. "You're getting off on this weird power trip?"

Cleo has no response other than her usual silent contempt. I continue scraping off dried cat crap that's stuck to the bottom of her litter box. Her wide green eyes are tuned to my every movement as she hovers in the doorway.

How is this my Friday night?

Lately, I like to trick myself into believing that Cleo's softened on her strict five-metre-radius, but right now I chalk the proximity up to her sadistic inner workings, and needing a front-row seat to me cleaning up her shit like some lesser being.

I stick my tongue out at her for personal satisfaction alone. Like always, Cleo has no response.

"Well, I want you to know that I totally made out with your dad, so I'm basically your step-mom now. How does that feel? I can ground you."

I don't know what that's supposed to mean, but it makes me feel a little better, at least, even though I'm scrubbing away at cat crap. And can't help my mind from drifting to the man in question, Noel's dark eyes still burning in the back of my mind.

Ever since I'd miraculously gotten hired at Viva La Breakfast, it seemed like we were always two seconds too early or two seconds too late and constantly missing each other. Not that I could complain, because suddenly I had two non-counterfeit twenty-dollar bills to rub together, no longer felt like a total disappointment to those 2 parents that are hopefully not looking too closely at me, and the imminent threat of eventual homelessness was a little less dire. But I couldn't help the tinge of disappointment that pulled inside of me when I'd pad back home after a tiring shift, only to find it empty inside.

I try to remind myself that his presence in my life is temporary at best, tied explicitly to Nat and Mark's wedding and nothing further. We're so coincidental it hurts.

And in that train of thought, making out with him again is probably one of the worst ideas I've ever had, and I thought bangs were a good idea for an entire year of my life.

I perk up, though, when I hear the doorknob jiggle, and can't help the silent expectation of a man in a suit on the other side. Instinctively, I tuck my dark hair behind my ear and push the litter box away from me.

Instead of Noel, though, bursting through the door is Natalya, blonde hair falling in soft curls down her back and her small figure wrapped up in a long, navy blue gown.

She does not look happy.

"What the fuck are you doing?"

I blink. "Cleaning cat shit?"

She's a flurry of movements, quickly crossing the room to pick me up off the floor and dragging me onto unsteady feet, muttering all the way about how she'd called like sixty times, goddamnit. Cleo's run off into the other room, abandoning me to be manhandled and verbally abused. I pull away with a frown.

"What are you freaking out about?" I ask, brows knit. "Also, not trying to butter you up here or anything, but you look really hot."

Nat rolls her eyes. "I look hot because Mark's cousin's birthday is today, and you promised me you would go like a month ago to convince all of Mark's family that you're totally amazing. Amazing enough that I didn't have to pick Mark's sister as my maid of honour. Which, as I've told you multiple times, Mark's mom has basically crucified me for with her shitty passive aggressive comments. Also, you're supposed to befriend the best man, like I've told you."

Her green eyes are narrowed, fixated and lethal, as she keeps a tight hold on my shoulders. All I can respond with is a sheepish grin.

I pointedly ignore the Noel portion, because who am I to say if I just hurdled right over the friend portion and went straight to the attempted fucking. "Oh yeah. That thing. But anyway, didn't I win them over at the brunch?" I ask, immediately wincing under Nat's dry look.

"You mean when you physically assaulted Noel?"

"But didn't I do that in like a charming way? You would say?"

Her face deadpans. "No. Now get your ass in there and change immediately because you have hearts to woo and I have jugs of expensive white wine to drink and forget this night ever happened."

I beam. "What are you, me?"

Nat snorts and shoves me towards the guest room, denying me the chance to protest before she's rifling through my closet and shooting dresses like projectiles towards my face. It's in record-breaking times that my hair's thrown over my shoulder in soft waves, eyelashes curled and coated, and I'm shoved into a soft black cocktail dress that's on the adventurous side of tasteful.

I shoot Nat a thumbs up while she gives me a once over, and when she meets my eye, she sighs. "Let's keep tonight light, okay?"

With a palm on my chest, I gasp. "What's that supposed to mean?"

"It means that you have a tendency to be Vika, and I'd like to keep the severe trauma tonight to a minimum, if possible."

There's an argument hovering on the tip of my tongue, but it dies when I see the tired sag of her shoulders. Instead, I shoot her an encouraging smile and link my arms with her, guiding us towards the door.

"Fine, fine," I sigh. "But I will stuff a disgusting amount of bacon wrapped anything in my mouth all night and no one can stop me."

Nat throws her head back, laughing, and pulls me closer to her. "I wouldn't dare get between you and your bacon."

Mark appears all knight in shining armor-like as he always does, and we both climb into a shiny black Camaro to be whisked away somewhere I didn't ask. He's too formal in a suit, dark hair pushed back and a gold Rolex clutched onto his wrist.

Despite the caviar and champagne dreams woven into his blood, Mark always seems to be more relaxed in a pair of scuffed up jeans, cheap beer in hand, and an arm wound snugly around Nat. Not that I can't objectively say he cleans up pretty well.

Nat's in the backseat with me, giving me another quick rundown of his entire extended family that I'm immediately forgetting as soon as it leaves her lips, like every other time she's gone through it. Still, the pressure's weighing on my shoulders, and an uncharacteristic anxiety brews along with my stomach acid.

I know I'm going to have to see Noel, but I'm not sure yet how.

We finally pull up to my disbelieving gasp of you guys got an entire hall for this birthday, are you serious, we literally got burritos and two bottles of tequila for mine.

Night's draped over the sky. I hold Nat a little too close to me, mouth permanently frozen and dropped in shock as we're swept inside. It's all twinkling chandeliers and pressed white table cloths, trays of hors d'oeuvres and flutes of champagne circling the floor. The room's bursting with the overwhelming presence of people, all reeking with wealth.

"Mark, are you secretly royalty, is that it? Are you actually a prince of some faraway land?" I ask, eyes wide and drinking in the extravagance.

"Not as far as I know." Mark shrugs with a laugh.

I'm still pathetically clutching onto Nat's arm.

Nat looks only slightly unbalanced by the culture shock, but she's quickly covering it up with a composed, glossy grin. I'd heard of these luxuries before, heard tales of the excessive and prodigal events that the Vanderbilt's basically threw too much money at, but a part of me just figured that she'd been exaggerating.

Now that I'm standing here, she wasn't exaggerating at all.

"Oh fuck, I forgot it."

Nat's eyes snap to mine, wide and panicked. "What?" she whispers, "What did you forget?"

"The solid gold brick up my ass."

Nat immediately relaxes, shooting me a heartless glare, but her mouth is twitching in the way where I can tell she's trying not to smile. Mark doesn't care, he's laughing next to me, as if he isn't inherently and genetically tied to everyone around us. I can't help but grin.

We're whisked further inside, and I swipe a caprese salad skewer with one hand and a glass of champagne in the other. There're plumes of expensive perfume in the air that I almost choke on, and the light bouncing off an arsenal of glittering jewels threatens to blind me.

The longer the atmosphere settles under my skin, the more out of place I am, reminded of the distinct fact that I'd been scraping cat shit less than two hours ago.

Still, I plaster on an inviting grin, clinking glasses and wishing Mark's cousin, and my new boss, a happy birthday when we see him. Seeing his familiar laugh lines and sharp grey eyes only further reminds me that I should be the one serving, not being served.

"It's been a whole twenty minutes and you haven't almost killed anyone, good job," Nat murmurs next to me when we finally break away from Mark's brother, her smile a little less tense. "Keep it up and I'll see what Mark can do about commandeering that bacon wrapped scallops tray."

"Mhmm," I mumble noncommittally, my eyes scanning the room. "Sounds good."

Nat pauses, stopping me with a touch on the shoulder. "Are you okay?"

I blink. "Hmm? Yeah. Just looking, this place is crazy. I thought you were lying before, but they really do swallow coal and shit diamonds here."

Nat smiles, but she doesn't appear wholly convinced by the way her eyes sweep across my face, searching. "Are you looking for Noel so that you don't accidentally murder him when you're not paying attention?"

Hearing his name out loud for the first time in days, back of my neck prickles. It's a ridiculous reaction to a name, and I'm immediately betrayed by the way that I stumble over my answer, choking back a few aborted words before spitting out an unsteady, "Um, kind of?" And then, more sure, "I just want to make sure that I don't break his leg when I'm not looking."

It seems like the more likely story.

Nat laughs, completely oblivious, and points to the other side of the room. "He's over there, I think?"

My gaze follows the direction, and in between an older woman with pearls and a tall, beefy man with a whisky glass in hand, stands Noel.

His hair is a little more tame than usual, lacking the usual tousle from his constant habit of running his hands through it, and he's wearing a sharp, charcoal grey suit that's almost melted to his skin. Even across the room I can see the stubble dusting his chin and, involuntarily, I think of it scraping along my throat. His dark eyes are hidden behind his thick-framed glasses, looking as cool and possessed as he always does.

Interestingly enough, he's not alone.

I pause, head tilting in curiosity as I take in a golden-faced brunette clasped on his arm. She's all cascading dark hair and mile-long legs, wrapped up in a glittery grey dress. Her head is thrown back as she laughs about something or another with her arm hooked around Noel's, just oozing poised relaxation.

"Who's that?" I ask, disregarding the semi-bitter taste that's in my mouth.

Always temporary, always coincidental, I remind myself.

Nat hums, shrugging. "Honestly, I have no idea. Maybe his girlfriend? Mark didn't say anything specific about a girlfriend, but he is bringing a plus one." She taps a French-tipped finger to her chin. "It's weird, but I honestly know next to nothing about him, Vi."

I swallow a sip of my champagne. "Oh."

Plus one's a pretty ambiguous term. Plus one could be anyone- an old friend, a distant cousin, or, I admit, a girlfriend. The conclusions are hovering on the tip of my tongue, but I swallow them down before they get too loud.

There's no need to assume, I remind myself. It doesn't even matter that they match or whatever. To a ridiculous degree. Like, red-carpet ready degree.

Whatever.

Mark waves Nat over, and she murmurs something my way that I don't catch before she disappears, leaving me to stand alone. I give her a noncommittal hum, my gaze still glued to the pair across the room, shattering any air of subtlety.

Then, under my piercing stare, Noel looks up.

Our gazes lock. His mouth twitches, eyes widening a fraction in a way that betrays he's caught off-guard, and I throw him a quick smile and a friendly wave. I'm ignoring the way that his dark eyes are raining tingles down my spine.

His gaze wavers on me for a moment, a quick up-and-down, and then he's back into the conversation in front of him.

For a second I'm frozen, brows furrowed, unsure if my mind is just playing tricks on me. A waitress with a tray of champagne brushes by, and I swiftly steal a flute. I frown.

Noel cannot be ignoring me.

chapter eleven

IT'S THREE GLASSES IN QUICK SUCCESSION and enough oysters to feed a small village that I finally admit- Noel is definitely ignoring me.

At first, I could convince myself that maybe, just maybe he didn't actually see me. It's a room that's practically alive with human presence, and I'd been swallowed up by the warmth of bodies and hum of conversation from the moment I stepped in. I'm sure we're both hovering on the right size of a decent buzz, so, the first time I give him the benefit of the doubt.

The fifth time, I do not.

The sixth time, I am pissed off.

I've been circling him for the past twenty minutes, brow arch more condescending every time I step into his peripherals and he, once again, looks away. By now he's staring so aggressively at the ceiling that he might fall in love with it, and he's barely even paying attention to the conversation playing out in front of him. Probably on the off chance I might be in his line of view beyond someone's shoulder, which, I am.

And he's not even smooth about it.

He's already downed two flutes of champagne, the rim of the glass reaching up to meet his lips every two to three seconds, and his mouth keeps twitching as if he's about to say something but never does. He's run his hand through his hair close to a thousand times, that angelic-faced woman still faithfully clasped around his arm.

I have no idea who she is, what relationship they have, but I refuse to play the fool and jump to conclusions. Even if they're practically gallivanting around the room like secret government prototypes for the rich and the famous.

Whatever.

Either way, after everything we've been through- at the most minimal degree, I deserve some sort of acknowledgement from Noel in public. A smile. A nod of the head. Something.

Waving a second time retrieves zero recognition on his part.

A middle finger the third time, strangely enough, gives me nothing.

Pointing to my eyes, and then to him with a look I'm sure lived in the gaze of Bruce Willis in every single Die Hard movie is absolutely useless.

There are a lot of things I am, I'm sure Nikki could write the next great American novel on it, but easily ignored is not one of them.

It's with a mounting frustration that can't be drowned in alcohol that I steal another glass, along with the arm of one of Mark's friends I vaguely recognize- Gerry, Gerard? Regardless, he's a source of conversation, since Nat and Mark are on the other side of the room entertaining Mark's a touch senile grandma, and I need conversation.

Or more realistically, a distraction.

And while I find no interest in basically anything that leaves his mouth, there's aging frat boy written all over him in the worst kind of way, his presence is enough to work with. We're strategically placed in Noel's peripherals, on my part of course, and judging by the way he's adjusting his tie, I know he sees us.

"Blake Bortles is killing my game- he's dragging down the entire team. At this rate, it'll all be over for me. I shouldn't have traded for Cousins. What a stupid fucking move."

I blink. "I'm sorry, what?"

"Fantasy football," Grant clarifies, grinning, as if that's supposed to mean anything.

Out of the corner of my eye, I can see we've temporarily caught Noel's attention, and I'm exploiting George's presence to the fullest extent. I throw my head back and laugh- bellowing and obnoxious, and graze his bicep. All of it is practiced in a way I've done time and time before.

Greg's smile is confused. "Hmm?"

"You're so funny," I reassure him, voice a pitch higher, beaming. "I seriously can't get enough of you."

This easily pleases him- he's all teeth and eyes flashing with a future that I'm sure has his palm pressed on the small of my back as he leads me out the doors. I'm not too concerned, I'm sure I'll be easily replaced by one of the many other girls that's giggling into her bubbly around the room.

What I'm more concerned with is the fact that Noel's mid-conversation with the older lady, and he is clearly not falling for any of my middle school tactics.

Which, fair enough. I was much more sly in high school.

I grin up at the man in front of me, and slowly my touch wanders from his bicep to his jawline, light and tempting. He doesn't seem the least bit bothered by this advancement as his eyes drag down my chest.

"You know, Glenn, I really think-"

"It's not G-"

"I really think," I cut him off, grin bright, "that you smell amazing. Really, I can't get enough. What is that?"

When I lean in, his eyes are sparkling, and his previous thought is long forgotten.

"It's Tom F-"

I don't give him the courtesy to finish his sentence as I press forward, capturing his lips with my own. They're soft and warm, and most importantly welcoming as my hand migrates to the back of his head, pulling him closer. As he's about to venture further, tongue brushing along my bottom lip, I pull away.

"Thank Tom for me, then," I murmur, smiling sweetly.

Gordon's too dazed to respond other than a slightly confused hum, still two-seconds in the past judging by the faint smile still playing on his mouth.

With a precarious swirl of emotions in my chest, my eyes shift over to Noel's direction just in time to see the dark-haired beauty on his arm reaching to whisper something in his ear. Instantly my excitement deflates.

He's not looking over here, instead, he's smiling- and it's one of the more genuine ones, I admit, albeit a tad begrudgingly. Sucking in a deep breath hardly quells the new-found tightness in my stomach.

Although they're only standing there, it feels as if they're parading their offensively good-looking selves around the room, digging the heels of their expensive Italian shoes all over my dignity.

There's a small part inside that reasons that I shouldn't even really care- even if he is ignoring me, who is he, to me, really? I don't even know the girl next to him, who he seems pretty close with from the way they move so naturally around one another.

But still, as my inhibitions loosen along with my limbs, I'm beginning to realize that I could.

Which is an awful revelation to have, especially when you're drunk.

They both fit so snugly within the aura of extravagance it makes me nauseous. He looks so perfectly in place it hurts, and as he grins down at the girl next to him, it's a reminder that somehow in Mark's apartment I'd felt like I'd had the upper hand, or at least equal playing ground, but here I'm realizing it was all an illusion. Here, on his home turf, I'm crumbling under the pressure.

"Hey, can I bum a smoke off you?" I ask Gideon, flat, not even bothering to play up my pseudo-smile.

Suddenly the game isn't as fun to play when you realize that you're playing by yourself.

He pauses, blinking a couple of times as if returning to the moment, and refocuses his gaze on me. "What?"

"A smoke," I echo, making a vague gesturing with my two fingers around my mouth. "Cigarette? Dart? Cancer stick?"

"Oh," he says, chuckling. Suddenly that grin that's all teeth and charm has found his face again, recalibrated and directed at me. "You know, a pretty girl like you shouldn't smoke."

"Mhmm," I hum noncommittally, forcing the edges of my mouth upward. "Can I bum off a smoke?"

He pauses and then laughs, low and husky in a way that feels wrong against my skin. There's a familiar itch in the back of my throat as he shakes one out for me.

As I reach for it, he pulls the cigarette back. "Want me to join you?" he asks, voice dripping with implications I'm all too familiar with.

"Give me two minutes, super quick, and I'll be right back." The lie rolls like velvet off my tongue.

He hesitates and then passes it over to me. "Don't make me wait too long."

"Wouldn't dream of it." I shoot him a small, heartless smile, and then I'm gone.

A part of me is guilty for suddenly changing my tune so rapidly it could give him whiplash, and leading him on for my own selfish needs, but I remedy it by reminding myself that he won't be sleeping alone tonight anyway.

And more importantly, I can't be in this room any longer.

I'm losing the battle to a strong craving for the sweet taste of escape, my nervous system shrieking red-alert under my skin. When the evening breeze gently touches my exposed skin, I shiver.

There's an underlying warmth in the air, coupling with the heat melting in my veins, and it's okay. I already breathe a little better. A little less anxious, less buzzing to get out of my own body.

With a much politer smile, I easily find someone with a lighter among my fellow degenerates outside. As I trail further into the darkness, I'm inhaling the carcinogenic smoke deep into my lungs with relief.

It's been months since I've had a smoke. A habit I always seem to pick back up whenever I've had a few too many drinks and Nat's lack of presence can't stop me.

The wisps dabble past my lips, and I lean my back against the cool brick wall with closed eyes, finally finding some kind of peace settled in my heart. My fingers calm their itching for release. The mingling of subtle music and conversation is muffled from inside, and the glow of the windows is too far to touch me out here.

I'm not sure how much time has passed, but the glow of orange has halfway devoured my cigarette when footsteps capture my attention. That sliver of calm I'd been holding onto is immediately consumed by a new bundle of nerves when a familiar silhouette draws closer. My pulse trips, and I look back to the ground.

He's, surprisingly, alone.

chapter twelve

WHEN I FINALLY SEE NOEL, I try to ignore the way my breath hitches in the back of my throat.

It's the closest I've seen him all night, close enough that my senses are seduced by the hints of fresh mint and sharp citrus that are agonizingly familiar notes of his cologne. Close enough to see the rise and fall of his breath underneath his charcoal suit, hands tucked into his pockets, the moon illuminating his face and drawing shadows in places that make my mouth water.

Close enough that I immediately avert my eyes and remind myself that I do not care.

There's a moment where it's quiet, and I can tell he's searching for my gaze, but I deny him the opportunity to catch it.

"You smoke?" he asks, finally breaking the tension, voice cool and collected.

I shrug nonchalantly, pointedly looking out into the sky. "That's what it seems like, I guess."

"You know, it's bad for you to smoke."

I finally drag my gaze up to meet his, blowing out a plume between my lips. "Thought you were a businessman, not a doctor."

He pauses, opens his mouth for a rebuttal, and then thinks better with a sigh. "Do you have an extra on you, at least?"

"A hypocritical one at that."

Despite the murmur under my breath, the dry look he pins me with tells me it doesn't go unheard. "I'm a little stressed, if you have to know."

"Stressed?" I echo, brows furrowed. "What about?"

"You."

Our gazes fuse in the midnight air, and I ignore the way it trickles down all the way to the base of my spine. His eyes are earnest in a way that I hadn't been suspecting, in a way that I couldn't have ever prepared for, and I'm caught off guard. When I catch myself, I swallow, and the sky steals my gaze once again.

"I'm honoured to have such an effect on you," I say, tapping the burning ember off my smoke. "But I don't have an extra, unfortunately. Giovanni was only nice enough to give me one. Guess we both didn't think I'd meet any friends out here."

Under the pale moonlight, I can see his mouth twitch. "Jason, you mean? And don't worry, I saw."

Suddenly the rest of Jason's sentence before I kissed him is making sense. I sniff and shake my head, bringing me back to the moment.

"You did, did you?" Mocking undertones drip from my words. "See, I thought maybe you just hadn't seen me, but it's great to hear you were just blatantly ignoring me. Reassuring. Thanks so much."

My smile is equal parts saccharine and lethal, and I pointedly blow another puff of smoke in his direction, if only to keep the violence between us on a second-hand level.

He threads his fingers through his hair. "I didn't mean to- it was just bad timing."

"Right," I drawl. "Timing, gotcha. And that would be the time to have basic human decency and respect? That time? I wasn't asking for you to profess your undying love to me, Noel, I was asking for a fucking wave. Acknowledgment that I'm an actual human being."

I swallow, a little harder than usual, and ignore the way my scalp prickles. There's the logical part of my brain that's already gobbling up his excuse and sweeping the rest under the rug, whispers of overreaction igniting in my synapses, but I can't ignore the way my stomach is twisting. There's too much unspoken in the way his gaze shifted from mine, and I can't seem to let it go.

A quiet floods between us, and it's a calm of the water's surface, a deceptive veil over all our messy, unspoken words that are clamouring underneath but not quite breaking through. We linger.

Neither of us has anything to say.

I drink in another drag from my cigarette and reluctantly meet his gaze

"It's... complicated."

His dark eyes are shining with something I don't want to admit to.

"Wow, okay," I scoff. "Have you considered trademarking that? You can't let that sort of originality slip through your fingers."

"I'm sorry, if anything. Truly, I am. I shouldn't have acted that way, and that was rude of me. I'm genuinely sorry."

His voice is soft, gentle, like smooth velvet against my skin. Within the darkness of his pupils, magnified by his black frames, I'm easily transported back to Mark's apartment, Mark's couch, his lips on mine. All the feelings come crashing back down too hard and too fast. I swallow them down.

I cross my arms over my chest, defiant. "How convenient, apology not accepted."

"How about if I give you ten thousand dollars?"

There's a small, muted smile that finds his face and it makes me want to pin him up against the wall and taste it.

I snort, eyes narrowing with a little less heart this time, biting back a smile. "Oh fuck you, my feelings are actually hurt here."

At the lack of venom in my voice, Noel visibly perks up, the perpetual crease in his brow finally softening.

"I know, I know, and I'm sorry. You don't deserve anyone making you feel like that. I'll make it up to you. I promise."

He takes a step closer, and for some reason, I can't stop myself from believing words that by anyone else I would scoff at. Somehow from his lips they're wrapping around my exposed shoulders like a fleece blanket. There's something in the way he hesitates before meeting my eye, and how he refuses to break when he finally does.

My drunken instincts have me wanting to bury myself in his neck, shamelessly nuzzle into his skin and drink in his cologne. The warmth in my chest is building and blossoming, and to stop myself from going too far, I hold out my smoke.

"Your apology is still not accepted, but you can take a drag if you so please."

The tension in his shoulders visibly relaxes, and he accepts my offer, shooting me a small smile. I pointedly keep my face deadpan, chewing on the inside of my cheek to keep myself from revealing too much.

"I didn't know you smoked," he says, bringing the cigarette between his lips.

I rub my arms fervently, hoping to generate any type of heat to combat the cool night air. "There's a lot of you don't know about me, Mr. Carlton."

"Mysterious," he muses.

A small laugh escapes my lips. "To be honest, I usually don't. Not anymore, at least, but I was terrible in high school. Skipping class and smoking under the bleachers are some great coping mechanisms for dead parents."

"It's also great for overbearing family and crushing expectations," he agrees, a stream of smoke whispering past his lips.

"Family?"

He nods, and despite my eyes already having adjusted to the low lighting of outside, his expression is marked by its usual stony countenance that I can't read too much into. I notice that the crease between his brows has appeared again, though.

"Lots of it, and with lots of opinions. One of them being my sister, Angelica, who was with me tonight," he explains, and then shoots me a sly look. "In case you were worried."

As the revelation comes to light, suddenly I'm cross-comparing features between the two of them- tanned skin, dark hair, long lashes, and I can't suppress the small touch of relief that relaxes my shoulders.

"What? Me? Worried? That you had a Victoria Secret angel on your arm?"

He gives a low chuckle and then passes the smoke back to me. "You're right, seemed a little busy with... what did you call him? Giovanni? Either way, I guess you and Jason were a little too busy to exchange names."

"What? You saw that?" My breath sharpens in a mocking gasp.

"Unfortunately. I must have forgotten. Are we in high school? Are you trying to make me jealous?" he asks, raising a brow.

I can tell he's fighting back a smile, and I can't help but laugh. Somehow, despite how silly it all seems now that the world is seeming a little sharper than it did fifteen minutes ago, the warmth in his tone forbids me from feeling stupid about it.

"I was trying to get your attention. Why, did it work?"

"Well, I'm here now, aren't I?"

He is, and somehow, despite all of my intentions, the carefully crafted knot that had accompanied me every time he'd avoid me in the hall is now unraveling under his gaze.

"I'm surprised you got away. It seemed like Angelica was clinging onto you pretty tightly all night."

He laughs, scratching at the back of his head. "She's not a fan of large crowds, and when she doesn't know anyone, she doesn't like to be left alone. I left her in the great care of Christian, though, so she'll be okay."

I draw in another drag from the smoke. "Well, either way, I'm glad. I would've been even more pissed if you had a girlfriend. I know I only have like, two morals or whatever, but one of them is no cheating." I hold out the bud of the cigarette to him, already on its last breath.

He shakes his head, and I nod, dropping the smoke from my fingers and the murdering it under my stiletto.

"What if we had started dating after you and I kissed?" he asks, tilting his head in curiosity.

I wrinkle my nose. "Yeah, but then that means I can't kiss you again, and that's no fun."

"You want to kiss me again?" His face reads genuinely surprised, ears unmistakeably dusting red.

I fix him with a measured look. "Don't play coy, it's not cute."

That might actually be a lie, but I bite it back, capturing my bottom lip with my teeth.

He laughs, scratching at the stubble on his jaw. "Well, as a twenty-nine-year-old man, cute wasn't what I was going for, honestly."

"Listen," I say. "Your best friend is a cat. Let's not aim too high here, just take what you can get."

This time I can't help the grin that finds its way on my face.

Noel bristles. "Mark is my best friend."

I roll my eyes. "Okay, yeah, sure. I may be dumb, but I'm not blind. You like that cat way more than Mark. More than anyone, really."

"You're not dumb," he argues, softly, and then, "It's, well, I need her. In some ways, she's all I have, okay?"

There's a beat of quiet between us, swallowed up by the midnight air, and suddenly I'm hyperaware of the flush that's still clinging to my cheeks from the many glasses of champagne. My pulse is heavy but steady, and I swallow when I see Noel's eyes shift to the darkness. There's too much saliva pooling on my tongue.

"Shouldn't you be going back inside? Isn't anyone going to miss you?" I ask, eyes falling to the asphalt beneath us.

A small smile pulls up the edge of his mouth, and he pushes his glasses up the bridge of his nose. "I'm okay right here, if that's all right with you."

"I don't mind the company," I admit.

He hasn't moved.

A shiver crawls down my spine.

"Are you going to make it up to me?" I ask, shattering the quiet. "For hurting my feelings. I didn't lie when I said I wasn't over it."

There's something on his face that I'm getting more and more familiar with, all of his intentions exposed within the heat of his gaze, dropping down my face and settling on my mouth. His eyes are searching along my skin, and there's a distinct weakness that floods my knees. Noel takes a step forward.

"How can I make it up to you?" he asks, but the way he runs his tongue along his top lip already knows.

I scoff. "What did I tell you about playing coy?"

Before he can reply, I'm pulling him closer by his tie and capturing his lips with my own. He's warm against my mouth in all the right ways, and he tastes like champagne and scallops, but also something uniquely Noel that I could get drunk off of, and I need more.

My fingers thread through his hair, and the heat of his palms snake down to settle decisively on my hips. I can barely keep up before his fingers are digging into my skin, dragging me flush against his torso and nudging me into the brick wall. His need mirrors my own, and all of our misplaced, sparing glances over the night are manifesting into a crescendo of his mouth against mine.

And I'm all fucking in.

Fingertips migrate down his chest, memorizing the feel of his body underneath them as he sucks soft reassurances down my jawline. My eyes flutter close as he finds a sweet spot just in the crook of my neck, grazing his teeth against my flesh in a way that has me panting, desperately grasping at him, wanting, needing more. There's a boldness to my hands as they drop further and then they're toying with his belt, just barely, but enough that Noel notices.

He pauses, issuing more of a whine than I'd like to admit from my lips. His glasses are slightly askew in a way that sparks the strangest things in me, and his breath is laboured, harmonizing with mine in short, sweet gasps. I go to kiss him again, but he pulls away.

I pout. "Why are you stopping?"

He swallows, and I'm transfixed by his Adam's apple dipping in his throat.

"I'm not going to do this here. I want to take my time with you."

I'm fucked.

chapter thirteen

MY LEGS ARE WOBBLING with all the grace of a newborn baby deer as I navigate about the restaurant, even more uncoordinated than usual and almost spilling hot coffee on not one but two unsuspecting old men. Thankfully both false alarms, since I have no doubt that most if not all the people who frequent Viva La Breakfast have brilliantly expensive lawyers on retainer, judging by the clear lack of attachment to their money.

Working for Christian still feels kind of Robin Hood-esque, and it's basically my moral right after years of down-on-my-luck fate to get some sort of compensation. I'm not doing this for me, but for all my fellow poor brethren out there.

Not that I'm sharing.

Although, I gave a rather gruff looking homeless man a dollar the other day, so, really. I've earned it.

As the clock finally strikes three and my shift draws to a close, a small sigh spills from my lips. All my muscles are burning from exertion, and as I stretch my arms high above my head, there's a delightful strain that brings a smile to my face. To be fair, though, it's not anything new.

I've been grinning like an idiot all day.

Nat notices, cocking a brow at me when I slide into the booth across from her and throw my apron on the table.

"What's got you in such a good mood? You think serving is ridiculously dull, it's been a week, but I know you're not that happy to see me," she says, eyes narrowed in suspicion, toying with the straw of her mint chocolate milkshake.

I give an innocent shrug and rummage through my pockets for my crumpled receipts, nonchalance betrayed by the grin that's plastered across my face. "Maybe I just had a good day? Now that I don't have to live off a diet of straight prison food."

She scoffs. "Are they serving Szechuan chicken in jail now?"

"Are you saying that all I eat is Chinese food? Racist, Nat. That's racist."

She rolls her eyes. "It's not racist if it's true. Now stop trying to change the topic- what are you so happy about? You fundamentally hate these people. You're never this happy unless there's trouble- and you're not getting out of this. Spill," she demands, a no-nonsense narrow of her eyes as she leans forward for intimidation factor.

I raise my brows, the picture of virtue as I smooth out receipts, pointedly avoiding her ruthless stare. "Am I not allowed to just be happy, Nat? Really?"

"No."

I snort, but as my mind inevitably trails back to dark eyes and thick-rimmed glasses, I can't help the unconscious curve of my lips. It's a silly habit that's been following me all day, and the bounce in my step is ridiculously high school of me, but I figure I'm not going to fight it. I shouldn't deny myself some sliver of happiness.

Although I reconsider when I meet Nat's eye.

"See!" she blurts out, pointing an accusing finger at me. "What is that? Vika, I swear, you better tell me or-"

"Promise me- promise you won't kill me, or else I won't tell you," I interrupt her with a small, unsure smile. I even fold my hands in front of me for good measure.

There's a pause, and then Nat's face drops. "What did you do?"

"Nothing!" I insist, throwing my hands up. "I promise, it's not as bad as you think. Just hear me out and don't stab me with your straw. It's... there's a man. A man who I have kissed." A pause. "Multiple times."

There's a beat, and then Nat's face immediately lights up, the sparkle in her green eyes instantly consuming all lingering suspicion. "What!" she gasps, reaching over the table and catching my wrist with a thwack, grinning all the while. "You've had a secret man this entire time and you haven't told me! Vika!"

I swat her away with a laugh. "I thought we promised no beating!"

"I promised nothing- anyway, talk. I considered killing you on grounds of terrible secret keeping, but I'll let it go. On the condition that you tell me everything," she orders, practically vibrating in her seat.

I take a moment to savour the grinning Nat for its sweet, momentary existence. His name lingers on the tip of my tongue, threatening to smash the entire scene to pieces like a wrecking ball teetering on the edge, waiting to fulfill its destructive destiny.

I hope at least that when I die, they realize I did it as a (mostly) honest woman.

"Well, that wasn't actually the reason I thought you were going to kill me," I murmur, distracting myself with a calculator and the numbers in front of me. "There might be something else."

Math can be very entertaining when it's between numbers or certain death.

She pauses, and without looking up, I can feel her eyes burning skeptical holes into me. "Vika, what did you do? Who is it?"

Her voice is dangerously low.

"It kind of happened on accident," I admit, refusing to meet her gaze. "You have to know, I didn't mean for it to be-"

"Who is it?"

"Why don't we go through some calming, deep breathing exercises first, yeah? Those are fun, just, do it with me, in-"

"Vika," she says, the tone of her voice a warning in itself. "Get on with it."

I meet her gaze, fold under the heat of it, and wince.

"Noel."

Silence swallows the air as his name hangs between us. I worry my bottom lip between my teeth, eyes darting from the receipts to Nat and back again, quick enough to make me dizzy. The quiet continues to weigh down on the both of us, only broken by Nat's long, loud slurp of her milkshake.

She finally lifts her head. "Nope."

I blink. "What?"

She shakes her head, brushing me off with a flighty wave of her hand. "Nope, no, you didn't just tell me you kissed Noel. You're making this up."

A frown tugs on the corner of my mouth.

"Nat, I'm serious. I'm not lying to you. I kissed Noel," I tell her, carefully reading her face. "And I'm pretty sure we're gonna bang tonight."

There's another pause, and then she gives a long, drawn out exhale.

"Vika, I'm telling you, please stop talking. I don't want to actually kill you, you know?" She gives an exhausted shrug, the telltale signs of assumed defeat that I know means only very bad, terrible things for myself.

Natalya Mikhailovya doesn't just back down. She wins.

"Nat, listen," I say, my voice more pleading than anything. "I swear-I didn't do it on purpose. Honestly, it just kind of... happened."

When I meet her gaze, bright with a naïve sort of hope, I get the Medusa of all stares back.

"Oh, don't pull that 'I accidentally fell on his dick' shit-'"

"We haven't actually slept together yet," I point out, but when I see Nat's face, I swiftly realize that it's not a helpful addition to the conversation. Like at all.

I quickly shut back up.

"What, did you slip? Lose your balance? Make a little oopsie-daisy into his pants?"

I roll my eyes. "Wow, you're such a good guesser. That's exactly what happened. Are you actually psychic?"

My desert-dry words don't seem to please Nat, whose lips are pursed, but I can't help myself. I'm not wearing white to her wedding or anything. Contrary to whatever Nat believes, I don't actually have a death wish, just a very pressing getting-laid wish that has Noel's name all over it.

Wishes that, if all goes to plan tonight, will most definitely be fulfilled.

Nat shakes her head. "No, Vika, no, you can't do it. I forbid you-forbid you!"

"You actually can't be my mom because she's dead, Nat, not sure if you remembered, so I can sleep with whoever I want."

She shoots me a deadpan look, but then her shoulders fall, and the fierce burning in her eyes relents. "Vika, I'm actually being serious here."

My brows knit. "When was I not serious?"

"Mark specifically told me that I shouldn't let you fuck with Noel. Mark. And Mark loves love, you know that. We watch Love Actually like, once a month on his request. And he doesn't want you guys together." There's a softness to her face that's lethal, the rest of her words unsaid but heard very loud and very clear.

The idea of disappointing Mark of all people is enough to immediately transport me into the depths of hell alongside lollipop-stealers and puppy-kickers, which is to say, a little disheartening.

I give a little huff. "What's everyone's deal? It's just a little fun. Is fun illegal now? I can't have just one nice thing?"

There's conflicted emotion written all over Nat's face as her eyes wander off. She opens her mouth, closes it, and opens it again.

"Noel, he's... well, um, apparently he gets... attached to things, is the best way I can put it. People included. At least, that's what Mark's told me. And we're just worried-," I restrain an eye roll from the very obvious we she's wielding like a weapon, "-that he's going to get attached, and you aren't."

"I'm gonna attach myself on that dick."

Nat shoots me a sharp glare. "I hate you."

I burst out laughing, which Nat doesn't join in, but I can see her fighting back a smile. Instead, she folds her arms over her chest and presses her mouth in a thin line, forcing her eyes to the window.

"Oh, come on," I say, the lilt of a chuckle still lingering in my voice. "We're both adults, and we both clearly understand that we're just letting off some steam. By making out, or whatever."

Nat raises a brow. "Oh, because you love to talk about your feelings? Did you guys draw up a contract or something? No box left unchecked?"

I buy myself some time for a somewhat intelligent reply by making a few pointed taps into my calculator, scribbling down the numbers. When I look back up, Nat's brow refuses to drop.

"Your precious wedding will be fine," I reassure her, giving a little encouraging pat on her wrist. "Won't it be better that we'll be getting along and no one will be getting sued? I'm kind of doing you a favour when you-"

"Shut up."

"Shutting up." I nod enthusiastically, grinning.

She meets my gaze, then sighs. "You already know we had to bump Stephen off the wedding party-"

"Oh my god," I groan. "Are you going to hold that over me forever? It's not my fault he fell in love with me. I can't help that I'm irresistible."

"Be resistible."

I give a helpless shrug. "You know that I kind of have a magical vagina that makes weird men fall in love with me. I'm not here to try and understand its magical powers. I just live them."

She pins me with a dry look. "Demystify your genitals and stay away from Noel. I don't know if you've realized it, but you kind of have a habit of..."

"Of?" I prompt.

She pauses, draws a deep breath, and crinkles her nose. I brace myself.

"Vika, you know that you kind of ruin things sometimes. People, specifically. It's just what you... do." Her eyes soften, and her gaze sweeps over me, gouging my reaction.

My scalp prickles, and a twisting finds my stomach. I divert my eyes back to the receipts in front of me. "That's mean, Nat," I murmur, voice lower than intended.

"I'm not trying to be."

I swallow, any chance at an argument crumbling before it can form around my lips. Instead, I sigh. "I was really excited about tonight, okay? We had like... Nat, I swear, it was a whole moment at Christian's birthday. And he said he was really busy, but I got a text this morning and I was... I don't know..."

"You were happy," she supplies, a sad smile on her face.

We're quiet for a moment, and then I clasp my hands together, a pout pushing out my bottom lip. "Can't I just have this one? I promise, I'll never hit on any of Mark's rich friends ever again. I'll become a nun around them. I'll wear the whole getup. Mother Vika. No matter how rich they are."

"Vika-"

"We're just going to have a little, no-strings-attached fun to get it out of our system- we'll probably only actually fuck once. Maybe twice. Not more than five, honest."

"Stop-"

"Please, please, please? Pretty please?" I continue my undignified pleading, shaking my clasped hands with the deepest frown I can muster. "I promise if your wedding isn't absolutely perfect I will ritualistically disembowel myself Samurai style. Cross my heart and hope to die. All of it."

Nat meets my gaze, narrowed in a challenge, but then she crumbles with a sigh. I restrain myself from jumping out of my seat.

"Grandpa duty."

"Yes!" I pump my fist in the air, and then freeze. "Wait- what?"

She takes another sip of her milkshake. "I won't say anything, but you're gonna be on grandpa duty all night for my wedding. Reception included. The entire time you're going to distract him away from all the other guests."

Memories of being practically detained by Nat's Russian grandpa's home country stories threaten to paralyze me all over again. I can tell by the devilish glint in her eyes that she knows I'm reliving it completely.

I give a tight nod of my head, forehead creased in pre-emptive pain. "All right. I'll do it. I'll do it for the dicking."

She beams. "Also, you're gonna have to share Bachelorette party duties with Mark's sister Cecilia."

"No!" I burst out, pointing a finger at her. "I refuse. Nat, she's the worst. She can't say penis without giggling like some Stepford wife. Bachelorette duty is my thing, I'm the maid of honour. Why do I have to share it?" I can't help the childish whine that forms around my voice.

Nat shrugs. "Then no Noel. I'll tell Mark. I'll shut it all down."

I open my mouth to argue, but only blow out air instead. The memory of Noel's lips moving against mine is still fresh, and it steals the words right from my mouth.

My cellphone is heavy in my pocket, holding Noel's first breach of contact with me all week- a text message, short, simple. I'm coming over today. Hope I can see you.

I can still feel his breath hot against my neck.

"Fine," I relent, rolling my eyes. "Okay, okay, I'll do it. I'll share bachelorette duty. Whatever. Don't tell Mark. Deal?"

Nat grins, nodding her head. "Deal. I'm just putting it out there- I'm dealing with zero of the cleanup when all of this goes terribly, horribly wrong. And I mean it, okay? I don't want to murder you, or have you commit ritualistic suicide, because finding a new best friend at this point would be way more trouble than it's worth. So don't fuck this up, alright?"

I snort. "Always the optimist."

She barks out a laugh, nudging her empty milkshake glass out of the way to press her elbows against the table and rest her chin on her palms. Her eyes are glistening with curiosity. "Now- back to what I first said. Tell me everything and tell me now."

It's the beginnings of twilight when I finally crash through Mark's apartment doors. Despite the months of free-loading, it still doesn't feel right to call it home. I remind myself that I need to start looking for a place to live soon, but that's all easily pushed to the back of my mind at the thought of Noel's coming visit.

I tried not to look too far into it when he'd dropped the bombshell of taking his time with me, and then not hearing from him for an entire week. I'd even asked Cleo if anything was wrong, but she just ignored me as always. Which is to say, I almost dropped my phone when a new number flashed across the screen and it was Noel of all people.

I'm sitting too straight on the couch, crossing and uncrossing my legs impatiently and barely even processing what's on the TV. My gaze keeps falling towards the door, only to snap back in shame to the screen seconds later, silently berating myself from pining like some middle school girl.

The wine I'd set on the coffee table calls for me, and I take a quick sip to settle my nerves.

I'm still trying to unravel the conundrum that is the relationship between my tripping pulse and Noel's face when I hear the doorknob fumbling, and I freeze.

I watch the doorknob turn, and then he's there, standing in front of me. Noel with his glasses and his stubble and his pressed suit, meeting my eye, winding me with just a glance.

"Noel, I-"

And then he's passed out on the floor.

chapter fourteen

"OKAY BUT I THINK he might actually be dead, Nat. I'm talking ninety, ninety-five percent sure here."

"Vika-"

"No, but I'm serious this time," I insist, leaning over the unconscious man and scanning his face for any hint of movement. There's nothing. I frown. "Nat, listen, he hasn't moved at all."

A tired sigh spills from the other end of the line. "You said that the last five times you called, and every time he's ended up moving. He's alive, just sleeping. People don't usually break into interpretive dance numbers when they're sleeping, if that's what you're waiting for."

I shift in my spot perched on the edge of the bed, close enough to get a good look, but enough distance that I won't disturb his sleep/death, the answer to whether he ends up moving in the next five minutes or not.

And the soup is only mildly helping.

I take another spoonful. "This time I'm serious-serious. I was the last person he saw before he fell unconscious. What if I'm too hot? What if it's my hotness that killed him?"

"Serious-serious."

I snort. "Okay, that was a joke, but really, I'm worried. He hasn't been moving. I'm genuinely concerned for his well-being here." I hold a breath as I peer over him again, only to be met with the same stoic, basically-dead expression.

The lack of frown on his face is the most upsetting thing, honestly.

"Is he breathing?" Nat asks, but the drawl in her voice already knows the answer.

I pause. The quiet is broken by soft, slight breaths. "... Yes," I answer, begrudgingly.

"Then he's fine. Didn't Mark say when he came by that this isn't really that rare? Noel overworked himself and has a small fever now. That's why he passed out. He needs to sleep it off," Nat reassures me for the umpteenth time, but I can't stop worrying at my bottom lip.

"Fine, fine, I'll believe you. Know that you'll be footing my therapy bill when he dies on my watch."

Nat laughs. "I promise. And Mark made some soup for him when he wakes up, right? So, it'll be fine. Unless- you aren't eating Noel's death-bed soup, are you, Vika?"

"... No."

Nat heaves a sigh, but it's betrayed by the lilt of a chuckle, and I can practically see her rolling her eyes from miles away. "Just make sure there's some left for the sick man when he wakes up, alright? You have a job now, you can't be stealing from the sickly."

"Can do!" I chirp, spooning up another mouthful of broth. "Still don't understand why I'm the one that has to nurse him back to health. I mean, I feel like I'm the most unqualified person in the current circle to do that. I've had to replace Nikki's fish like three different times."

"Well, Mark has to stay at the office for a project because of his awful boss, and I have to entertain Mark's sister for this pre-bridal shower-whatever. Unless, do you want to switch with me?"

The thought of Mark's sister, Cecilia, and her offensively nasal voice that still haunts the corners of my darkest nightmares causes me to pull a face. It doesn't help that not getting the maid of honour position over Nat's longest and closest friend apparently means Cecilia's entitled to a mountain of passive aggressive comments, so I have to suppress a gag at the thought of spending more than five minutes with her.

"I think I was born to be a nurse, honestly."

Nat snorts. "That's what I thought."

Muffled in the background, I can hear something surprisingly insincere form around a, "Who's that? Is that Vika? Tell her I said hi and that I wish she could've come," and my face immediately drops.

"Tell Cecilia to suck my dick."

"Vika says hi back!" Nat supplies instead, her voice uncharacteristically bright and cheery. I fight back a laugh. There's a pause, and a small groan trickles from the other end. "That offer still stands, by the way. Feel free to save me from this- yes, I'll be right in! Don't mind me!"

"Oh, what was that? I think Noel's moving! Oh man, gotta go! See you later! Have fun!"

Nat laughs as I click off the phone, and once again I'm surrounded by a thick silence in the room. I carefully place the soup on the floor, then lean over Noel's resting figure. His lips are parted. The small rise and fall of his chest reveals some kind of sentience, but I can't soothe the gnawing worry that's been eating away at me since he'd dropped almost-dead in the doorway.

Despite everyone's casual attitude, I can't convince myself that I shouldn't be anxious. Especially when I'd slapped him once, maybe twice if cameras were watching, and I'd gotten no response at all.

Was that weird of me? That instantaneous fainting makes me the smallest bit alarmed for his safety?

With my breath hitched in my throat, I gingerly place the back of my hand against his forehead. It's warm to the touch. A frown tugs on the edges of my mouth, the burning of his skin only further spurring my concern.

It's strange seeing him more helpless than I ever have before, a stark contrast to his usual cool and composed self. A part of me wonders if overworking himself is the reason he hasn't been around the condo.

I can't decide if I want to slap him upside the head or tuck him in.

As I move to pull away, movement passes over his features, and I freeze. His lashes flutter open, and he draws a deep breath, dazed brown eyes reaching mine. "Vika?" he murmurs, brows pinched in confusion.

I retract my hand, curling it into a fist with wide eyes. "Sorry, I didn't mean- I'll go. Rest up. You should be sleeping."

He seizes a grip on my wrist and pulls my hand back. His eyes are hooded, still lingering in the dimension between sleep and awake, but they're earnest in the way that warms something in my chest.

"Stay?" he asks, his voice soft and painfully vulnerable.

I blink, only air passing through my mouth when it parts for an answer. Then his eyes are drifting close and he's gently snoring once again before I can give him any reply.

The hold he has on me relaxes, arms falling back to his sides, but I'm still paralyzed. There's a beat of silence where I'm unsure if even breathing is okay. Shock is thick like cement in all my veins, but it slowly melts away as I look down to Noel's sleeping face.

When I'm almost absolutely sure that Noel hasn't been abducted by even weirder aliens than his usual species, a small sigh escapes my lips, and I slowly withdraw my hand. The sound of his voice, small and unsure, is still echoing in my mind.

I take an uneasy glance to the door, to the laptop I'd brought in, and then to Noel once again. The logical part of my brain reasons that fever speak is like vodka on the tongue, but the precarious swirl of emotion in my throat disagrees, and I sigh again.

"Looks like it's a Project Runway marathon type of night," I say to no one in particular.

I settle myself with my back against the bed, a fleece blanket wrapped around me. There's a good twenty minutes of me trying to battle between my budding concern for his life and the selfish voice of disappointment, how this wasn't playing out the way that I'd originally planned the night to go. Both of these thoughts are weighing on my shoulders like globe-shaped boulders, so I concentrate on my laptop screen instead, learning the riveting difference between red and blood orange.

I'm not sure when the afternoon light surrenders to the softness of twilight, or before night ends up devouring the sky, but then I'm rubbing the sleep out of my eyes with a yawn, head lolling back and legs falling asleep sporadically, and I'm out.

When my senses finally return, there's an irritating trickle of light peeking through the blinds. Unfortunately for me, it's landing straight on my face and demanding my full attention. My eyelids are heavy, straining against any effort of consciousness, especially with the softness that's reaching up to cup my cheek, but eventually I yield to the light.

I stretch, and when I finally blink awake, it dawns on me that while I'm still in Mark's room, I'm definitely not on Mark's hardwood floors. A goose-feathered pillow and plush duvet are soft underneath me, and I'm all alone.

Panic bursts in my chest. I shoot up into a sitting position, whipping my gaze around the room.

"Noel?" I call out tentatively.

Footsteps respond to my question, and suddenly Noel's standing in the doorway, taking a sip of the soup held in his hands. His dark hair is mussed, but the red tinge seems to have faded from his cheeks.

He's seemed to have found his glasses that I'd gingerly placed on the end table, miraculously unharmed by his fall. As my gaze drags along him for a quick wellness check, I have to do a double-take.

"Sweatpants?"

His gaze drops to light gray sweatpants and bare feet, his mouth twitching. "They're Mark's? I do wear other clothes than dress shirts, if that's what you're asking," he says, flat stare meeting my disbelief as he pushes his glasses up. "Contrary to your constant assertions, I'm not actually a robot."

I frown. "Looks like the damage was worse than I thought. And it's aliens, not robots, get it right Noel."

Despite the drawl of my voice, and the scoff from Noel that follows, I can't help the soothing waves of relief that are coursing through me at the sight of him standing on his own two feet, seemingly okay, not dead at least. It's a far-cry from the man who'd held my wrist and asked me to stay, but it's oceans closer to the Noel I know.

"Sleep okay?" he asks, and I'm slightly taken aback by how sincere it sounds.

"I'd recommend you dying somewhere a lot comfier next time. May I suggest a cloud, or a bouncy castle? Noel Guard Duty is some pretty heavy duty stuff." I roll my shoulders, a lion-like yawn spilling from my lips as I stretch. I can only imagine the mascara smudges under my eyes. "I accept payments only in cash. And as we already know, my time isn't cheap."

He pauses, eyes widening. "Oh. Um, how much should I give you?"

I blink and give a very lady-like snort. He shifts uncomfortably, refusing to meet my gaze. A tinge of pink that has nothing to do with a fever crosses his cheeks.

It's ridiculous that I have to remind myself that I probably shouldn't jump the man who was almost dead less than twelve hours ago.

"Jesus Christ, a thank you will suffice, Noel. We'll talk numbers later." I beam.

"You didn't have to stay the entire time. I didn't mean to- it happens all the time. Big presentation. Lack of sleep." He takes another sip of his soup and averts his eyes. "Sorry if I scared you."

"Sorry? Is that your very bad way of saying thank you? Listen, it's easy. Say it with me. Thank you. You're the best, Vika. I'm writing you into my will right now, Vika. Now repeat that back to me."

The endearing and fumbling shame has evaporated now, his usual dry look of discontent returning with full force as he rolls his eyes at me. "There's some leftover soup in the kitchen, if you feel inclined. Watching garbage TV must really take a toll on you."

I'm convinced he really did turn into a different person for a second back there, when he'd tugged so weakly on my wrist. He looks too pleased with himself to ever be that vulnerable.

"First of all, Project Runway is an art form. Second of all, I changed my mind. You can repay me by feeding me soup in bed. I'm waiting.

You owe me. I'm talking spoon-fed here." I fold my arms over my chest and shift to get more comfortable in my seat, grinning.

The corner of Noel's mouth ticks upward. "I'll leave a hundred on the counter. Next to the soup. Which you will be getting yourself."

Before I can say anything, he and his pretentiously cocked brow have disappeared from the doorway and down the hall. A few aborted, half-human noises leave my mouth.

"Come on, Noel! I deserve compensation! Hand feeding me isn't too much to ask! Noel! Noel? .... Were you serious about that hundred dollars, though?"

When I don't get any response in return, I heave a sigh and drag myself from the comforts of Mark's bed to the shower. As I'd expected, a quick glance in the mirror reveals chaotic bedhead and raccoon eyes. A quick flash of Noel from the other night crosses my mind, whispering promises into my ear that made my knees weak, and then immediately dissolves.

I'm wholly convinced that this is all Nikki's voodoo juju and I'm never going to get laid again. All because I killed a couple of her goldfish.

That hundred dollars better be an actual thing.

When I've finally cleaned myself up to semi-presentable standards, I try to convince myself not all hope is lost as I swipe a few coats of mascara, and find Noel lounging in the living room. There's a computer on his lap instead of Cleo and an empty bowl of soup left on the coffee table. He doesn't hear me until I dump myself on the couch next to him.

"There was no money in the kitchen, by the way. I nursed you back to health, and this is the thanks I get? Lies? Deception?"

He shoots me a measured look. "I thought we were over trying to extort me for money."

"But I actually earned it this time! You were all like, Vika, don't leave me, I'm so weak, I need you to nurse me back to health. You even grabbed my wrist like a little puppy or something. It was adorable," I tell him, smirking as I shift closer.

His eyes widen "I did not."

"After you even tried to have sex with me. I had to fight you off me, like damn, I didn't know you were that into me, Noel. If you wanted some, you could've just asked nicely."

Okay, maybe the voodoo juju is just the regular kind of karma, but Noel's horrified face might be one of the funniest things I've ever seen in my entire life.

His mouth is gaping. "I did not."

It's 0.2 seconds before I'm crumbling into laughter and waving him off, barely getting a word out, actually snorting like a pig at one point. "Okay, I'm sorry. The second part wasn't true. I did nurse you back to health, and you did ask me to stay by your side, but I promise it was a very G-rated ordeal. But you were seriously concerned there for a second, oh my. I'm sorry to generate that nightmare fuel for you."

I'm still laughing when Noel pauses, pinching his brows and sizing me up. "Vika-"

"Yes, I did snort like a pig. Listen, my body makes noises sometimes, and we all gotta live with it."

"I'm not disturbed by touching you, I'm disturbed by doing it half asleep. Vika, if I'm going to touch you, I want to remember it."

The end of my sentence dies on my lips, and suddenly I'm being consumed by Noel's dark gaze, overwhelming me all at once. If those words had been said by anyone else, I'm sure I would've laughed in their faces, but I can barely catch my breath now. I wonder if fevers are contagious as a flush crawls up my neck.

"Then touch me."

I swallow, hard, and meet his gaze.

And then he does.

chapter fifteen

THE SECONDS ARE MINUTES are millennia are just heartbeats. The sound of my breath, shallow and short, is a manifestation of my pulse thrumming wildly in my chest. Time has slowed down almost to a standstill. All the noise of the outside world is swallowed up by my sharp intake of breath. Quiet, silent, static. Everything but him and me ceases to exist.

And then I'm kissing him, and the entire world comes crashing back down in roaring technicolour.

Suddenly I'm too aware of the heat of his skin. The promise of his touch materializes in the way that his hand cups my jaw and his nose brushes against mine. His eyes are closed, lashes sweeping down to his cheeks, but I can feel the scorching of his pupils trickling down my spine.

My mind and body haven't quite synced up yet.

My hands move in a way that's muscle memory of every midnight fantasy I'd devised up in my head, my mind too dizzy from trying to piece together reality and Noel's mouth coexisting as one to even begin to catch up. There's no alcohol on my breath, but somehow all my senses are dazed, numb, and on fire all at once.

His lips are soft and tentative against mine, revealing hints of hesitation that I'm too quick to annihilate as I climb into his lap. His laptop has been shoved off to the side and long forgotten. I'm almost flattered, but I'm more focused on slowly lifting his glasses off, placing them to the side and stealing his undivided attention.

There's a plunge in my stomach that is always two steps behind what my hands have already claimed. His surprise is betrayed by the slight flutter of his eyes and the small tense of his hands, but slowly dissolves as I press into him, deepening the kiss, quietly asking for more.

"What was that you'd said before? I want to take my time with you?" I murmur with a smirk tugging on the corner of my mouth, pulling back to meet his gaze.

His eyes widen a fraction. "Christ, you remember that?"

"Remember?" I scoff, shifting in his lap, the friction igniting exhilarating sparks through all of my veins. "You're blushing as if I haven't been touching myself to the memory for weeks. You're not breaking your promise, are you?"

He swallows, but I can't miss the way his hands travel down to curl around my hips, barely dipping under my shirt in a way that makes my entire body hum. There's a tinge to his cheeks that I hope isn't remnants of fever, and when he opens his mouth for a rebuttal, all I can focus on is his bottom lip shining all kiss-bitten and just begging to be pulled between my teeth.

Honestly, if teasing him wasn't so fun, I wouldn't be able to keep my mouth off him.

"At this point, I don't think I could," he admits with a breathless quality to his voice that threatens to wind me. "I mean, I wanted to, you know, something more than this but Christ, stop squirming around so much or you're going to kill me."

Hands hooked around his neck, I tilt my head, capturing his gaze with a cocked brow. "More than this? Noel, I hope you know we're only getting started."

I rock into him with an indulgent grin, the thin layers of fabric between us leaving little to the imagination. A low, hoarse noise sounds in the back of his throat that I would've never expected from him but somehow feels like molasses dribbling down to my tailbone.

"I meant- Vika, I mean on Mark's couch, you haven't had breakfast yet, sweatpants, I-"

"Noel," I cut him off with a sigh. "I'm flattered, really, that you're so concerned about my breakfast, it's very cute, but it's fine. This isn't The Notebook, and I don't think your friend digging into my thigh really cares all that much."

He turns his head to the side, pointedly avoiding my gaze, and the way that his cheeks dust darker melts something inside of me. Still, his hands are still pressing tightly into my hips in a way that says he hasn't surrendered yet, hopefully something more than curiosity keeping him compliant underneath me.

And I can't ignore the genuine sentiments that are hiding behind my words, of how resoundingly right it is to be straddling him on this couch, in this apartment, completely hidden away from the world. The only currency that exists here is our feather-light touches, and that's all I need in this moment between the two of us.

In the back of my mind plays a reel of the birthday party we'd been to, of those sparkling chandeliers and bubbling champagne flutes and an entire life that seemed built into Noel's blood but always barely out of reach for mine. And in the same breath, Noel too. As if I'd been sentenced to never break anything more than being a spectator, a bystander, exiled to the outside.

But here, almost naked in more ways than just skin, suddenly it's not so far. He's more real to me than he's ever been, the way goose-bumps rise to my touch, the way his breath hitches in his throat, he's so human it hurts. Suddenly that overwhelming unsaid hierarchy suffocating the memory of that night dissolves in our kiss.

Also, he's really fucking hot. So there's that.

"Listen, I was made promises, and I'm here to collect," I murmur, smirking as I gently take his chin between my fingers and turn him back towards me, demanding his gaze. "Tell me you don't want this. Tell me you want me to stop, and it's done."

My words are dripping confidence, but I can't help the minuscule, nagging little thought in the back of my mind that he might. That maybe we aren't as far away from the entire world as I feel.

In a move that honestly surprises me, Noel's hand lifts to curl around my jaw, those fingers I'd always watch lacing through Cleo's spotted fur now threading through my hair. I barely keep myself from entirely unwinding underneath his touch.

"Do you know why I passed out when I came here?"

My brows pinch, unsure of where he's taking this, but with the warmth of his palm bleeding against my skin, I have no objections. "Uh, 'cause you overworked yourself?" I haphazard, my voice seemingly faraway.

"Yeah, but- I can't believe I'm saying this." He draws a deep breath, and somehow, unconsciously, I'm holding my breath too. "Vika, I wanted to see you. I came straight from work here as soon as I was done because I couldn't stop thinking about you all week. It's been killing me trying to stay away. Almost literally."

His burning gaze completely devours mine and immediately steals the air from my lungs. It's too much, there's too much drowning in his coffee dark eyes, and I'm drowning in it too.

I have no answer other than to pull him in for another kiss, wet and hot and frantic, needy in a way that I'd never admit to. I'm chasing his mouth with a hunger that's scorching too hot in my belly, twisting and coiling as he tightens his grip on my hair.

I can feel his movements resonating in the way he's stirring underneath me, against me, stiff to the touch. Any uncertainty has vanished between us, replaced only with the all-consuming need to get closer.

Wandering fingertips dip under the waistband of his pants, but our kiss doesn't break, refuses to. The heat of his mouth drips all the way between my thighs in a rain of sparks that have me completely unwinding. The blood's pumping in my ears in a way has a moan building in my throat and he's barely even touched me.

I'm hindered by silk, and a smirk once again toys on my lips as I gently pull down his sweatpants to reveal a smooth, glossy flash of cherry red. It's completely unexpected but thrills me like no other pair of boxers ever have in my entire life.

"Silk boxers?" I muse, mouthing the words into skin under his ear. "Well, aren't you a regular Casanova."

"They're comf- Christ, Vika," he breathes out, the words dying from his lips.

"Hmm?" I murmur, a little too cocky for my own good as I pepper kisses down his jawline. "C'mon, you can tell me."

His head falls back, exposing the Adam's apple of his neck and soliciting all sorts of filthy thoughts running through my mind. There's a new boldness spurred by the unraveling of Noel underneath my touch, completely at my mercy.

And somehow what threatens to obliterate me are the soft reassurances he's still rubbing into my hips in small circles, gentle but still enough to remind of his presence, remind me of something I'm not sure I can quite swallow. It's almost enough to be unfamiliar, but I never want him to stop.

"Shouldn't-" he says, but his breath catches and I can barely contain myself, to the point where when he does manage to lift his head, slight hints of composure returning, I'm almost disappointed. "Wasn't I supposed to be the one fulfilling promises?"

I tilt my head, amused, as I place another kiss on the corner of his mouth. "Oh, is this not good enough for you? Should I change it up?"

"Vika- I mean, fuck, you're going to be a death of me, you know that?"

When I meet his gaze, I'm beaming. "Is that a no?"

"No-"

"No?" I raise my brows.

"I- let me, when I make a promise, I tend to keep it," he says, but I'm barely listening as both of his hands migrate from my hips to my neck, cupping my jaw and pulling me closer so he can capture my mouth into a kiss. Everything but the warmth of his mouth is long forgotten. When he pulls away, he's smiling. "Would you let me keep it?"

These sorts of things leaving his mouth should be fucking illegal.

I all but keen into him, nodding my head as all the impatient and eager words collect too quickly in my throat before I can even get my mouth around them. He chuckles, deep in a way I've never felt deep.

Then he's nudging me off, and I'm missing his warmth before I'm reluctantly moved to my back. I meet his gaze. His pupils are blown, wide and dark, and the red tinge is still clinging to his cheeks in a way that echoes throughout my entire body.

I've never seen Noel so affected. And it could, quite possibly, be one of the hottest things in the world.

He's hovering over me, caging me in under the couch, but I can't even begin to make sense of it before his hands are travelling down, over and under and leaving a sensory fire in their wake.

His touch is slow, wandering, as if he's committing every moment to memory. It drifts up from my neck, to my jaw, to my cheekbone.

He's barely brushing against my lips in a way that can only be described as a tease. Noel pauses, and I can see a look of consideration cross over his features before he's gently pressing his thumb along my bottom lip and I'm gone.

Without breaking eye contact, his thumb falls into my mouth, so soft it almost hurts, and I'm readily running my tongue along his skin. It's an uncharted territory between us, but I can't deny that it has my stomach and thighs tightening in eager approval, a faint hum sounding in the back of my throat.

He seems almost as mesmerized with it as I am, though, judging by his breath hitching audibly in his throat.

Noel blinks, and only moves his thumb to replace it with his mouth, warm and inviting and shooting tingles down every inch of my body. "Was this was you were thinking about all week?" he asks, and for a moment I have to remind myself to breathe.

"Better," I admit.

He chuckles, dropping another kiss on my lips as his hands stray farther down, dipping under my shirt only to climb back up to my bra, which I'm surprised I'm still wearing. My chest is heaving and I realize that we haven't even had the decency to get undressed yet, our clothes a wrinkled mess between us, but I don't mind. "You'll have to show me," he says.

Somehow, in this apartment, I've got all the time in the world. There's no deadline to learning every contour and crevice of his body, or of him discovering mine. Time's a consequence of an outside world that can't touch us.

chapter sixteen

"I'M SO SORRY, BABY. I didn't mean it, I promise. Forgive me, please, I don't even know what I was thinking."

I understand in a karmic sense that sure, I've lived a less than perfect life. I've accidentally killed a fish here and there. I've littered. I buy child's tickets at the movie theatre and hope that the jaded fifteen-year-old doesn't care too closely- and they never do. My general juju probably has a few stains here and there.

Honestly, I get it.

But this is ridiculous.

"Please look at me, I'm sorry. I wasn't thinking. I was just- please."

My lips press into a thin, concentrated line as irritation licks up my rib cage, iron-hot and corrosive. It's only growing stronger the longer I hear his voice, pleading and desperate, muffled from the other room. It's a complete 180 from the low, throaty whispers that had been tantalizing my senses only twenty minutes ago, the sweet promises he'd been pressing into my skin- gone. Vanished. Completely dissolved.

And instead, this.

"Baby, please look at me. I'll do anything. I promise it won't happen again."

Noel is an alien. That is literally the only explanation that makes sense.

"Nat, I swear to god, he's been talking to the cat for the past ten minutes and he keeps calling it baby. Baby. Why didn't you talk me out of this? Why did you let me do this?"

The cackling that sounds from my cellphone threatens to break my eardrums.

Which, at this point, might be a welcome addition to my life.

"What kind of weird shit did you guys get up to? How badly could you have possibly scarred this cat? Wait- do I even want to know? Think hard before you answer. I know you can't afford my therapy bills," Nat says, but any sense of sincerity is betrayed by her sadistic laughter.

My narrow gaze fixates on the ceiling of my room, where I'd escaped to after Noel had realized Cleo was watching us from the corner (the pervert). I was hoping that Noel and I could go farther, explore deeper, finally breach whatever we'd been tiptoeing around this entire time and adventure to amazing, orgasmic faraway lands.

Or just get somewhere that didn't end up with me in my bedroom, alone, and talking to Nat on the phone.

Honestly, I wish any man harboured even half the amount of passion for me that Noel did for that damned demon cat.

"It was all strictly hand stuff! I did dirtier things when I was a junior in high!" I huff, heaving myself up into a sitting position and shifting my glare to the doorway where pathetic cooing could still be heard from the other side. "He's acting as if we stole her innocence or something."

"Well, clearly you did, Vika. It sounds like she won't ever be the same again after this."

I roll my eyes. "She's a cat."

"A traumatized cat," Nat corrects me with an unnerving amount of enthusiasm.

I groan, again. "Everyone around me is awful and I hate all of you. I have enough on my plate as it is with Dr. Doolittle over here, so I'm hanging up on you. Try to be less of the worst next time I call you in my time of need. Goodbye."

Her only response is, once again, laughter. I think I hear the beginnings of a, "Wait, don't forget-" but then I've already clicked off and dropped my phone on the comforter, wondering if there's a limit to the amount I can roll my eyes before they roll right out of my head.

At least that would've saved me from the scene I find when I trek back into the living room.

"Oh my god, it's a cat," I grumble, crossing my arms over my chest and leaning against the doorframe.

Noel barely spares me a glance, his eyes flickering for a moment to narrow on me before they're back on Cleo again, softened and pleading. He's still dressed casual in his sweatpants and loose t-shirt, an aesthetic that makes me stare a second too long even after all this time, and his hair is mussed from all the times my fingers had run through it.

He's ridiculous as he fixes his glasses, frowning at Cleo and crouched in the middle of the floor. She's perched in the corner, chin up, eyes as callous as they've ever been.

I hardly see a difference, but Noel's acting as if she's having a hysterical breakdown.

"She has feelings," he says, voice clipped.

"Cats don't have feelings."

Noel sighs, and lifts to his feet, brushing his hands together. "I don't think you have the credentials to make that judgement." His gaze shifts to me, deadpan as usual.

I raise a brow. "The credentials of common sense?"

"You and common sense are a debatable pair."

Instinctively, my mouth opens to protest, but then after taking another survey of my circumstances, closes again. I sigh. "Clearly, if I'm in this situation."

Noel pauses, brows pinching thoughtfully before he takes a few steps forward, the couch no longer a safe medium between us. My head tilts in curiosity as a small, unreadable smile tugs on the corner of his mouth.

"This situation? It didn't seem like you were complaining before." He pauses two steps away, the closest we've been since he'd shoved me off him, rough in all the ways I did not want.

I scoff. "Before you were paying more attention to me than the cat."

"Are you jealous of the cat?"

I hesitate, swallowing my defensive instincts when I see Noel almost beaming, the creases of worry that seem permanently engraved between his brows miraculously softened. The edge of his mouth is still hovering in that half-hearted smirk, and all I can muster is a shrug.

"When it's interfering with my ability to get some, I'm gonna have to go for a shameless, resounding yes. Absolutely. Of course. All of the above," I admit, slapping both palms against my cheeks and pulling the skin down, barely believing the words that are coming out of my own mouth.

I wonder if pleading insanity due to sexual frustration is a reasonable defense in court.

Noel's smile almost upgrades to a full-blown grin, but then he's coughing into his fist and clearing his throat, as if he's as surprised as I am, despite asking in the first place. "Well, you're going to have to hold back until Cleopatra's gotten over it."

I almost choke. "Wait- what, are you serious?"

"I'm completely serious."

My jaw hangs open for a moment, quicker than my brain that's still processing. "You're seriously not going to have sex with me until I get this cat's blessing?"

Noel blinks. "Well, I will-"

I breathe out a generous sigh of relief. "Thank god."

"Not in this apartment," he continues, unfazed by my aborted half-human choking noises, "obviously."

"Obviously?" I echo, "Jesus Christ. I cannot believe that this is my life right now. Tell me this is a joke. Please- please tell me that you're joking. Is this a bit? Are you doing a bit right now?"

Noel's face pinches, a defensive frown weighing down his mouth. "She's sensitive."

"She's a cat!"

"Don't say that about her. I understand you're upset, but there's no reason to take it out on her."

The earnest concern that's flashing in his dark eyes has me both wanted to rip out my hair and kiss him all at once in a strange mixture of emotion I'm getting more and more familiar with the longer I spend time with Noel.

I heave another sigh, cheeks puffing as I take a moment to, once again, wonder if there's any chance of saving my poor karma ratios or if I've lost all hope of that.

"How do I still want to sleep with you?" I murmur, mostly to myself, while carding a hand through my hair.

Noel visually perks up. "You still want to sleep with me?"

Something in my chest warms at the unusually hopeful tone in his voice.

I shrug. "Unfortunately."

He grins, and takes a step towards me that has something hopeful hovering in the back of my throat, but Cleo takes the opportunity to dart into the hallway and all attention on me is lost. My face drops as Noel immediately pivots towards the cat's disappearance and follows her with quick steps, causing me to throw my hands up in defeat and groan.

"I'm a good person, okay? I could be like, way worse. I could kill people," I complain, loudly, to no one in particular.

I'm convinced at this point that Nikki must have done some sort of voodoo magic. For a moment, my mind experiments with the idea of finally paying her back for all those missed month's rent, now that I have at least some money to my name, but I remember that I have to pay for first and last month's rent of the new place I'm inevitably going to get, so maybe another month or two won't hurt. She's doing fine, I tell myself, and find distraction in following Noel.

"Is this some kind of weird foreplay for you? Is this why you keep doing this?" I ask, turning on my heel and leaning against the doorway.

Noel's sitting on Mark's bed, a brush in hand as he's gently sweeping through Cleo's spotted fur, and looking up at me. "I don't know what you mean."

"Come on, is this turning you on or something? Withholding from me? That's the only reasonable explanation here."

Noel's head shifts back, confusion creasing his brow. "This is about Cleopatra."

"What about some making out, at least? Over the clothes. PG-rated and everything," I propose, ignoring the hope saturated in my words, too busy drowning in the memory of him pressed up against me. I bat my eyes in a way I hope is convincing. "I promise, I'll keep my hands to myself. Mostly."

A small smile breaks out across his face. "Tempting offer, but not in this apartment."

"Noel," I whine, "Are you seriously going to make me beg? Unles s... are you a virgin? Is that it?"

My jaw drops with a quick gasp as I consider the possibility, the shock only swelling when I see a distinctive red burn at the tips of his ears.

"No," he blurts, stressing the vowel out and shooting me a sharp stare. "I was in a four-year relationship, thank you very much."

I pause and exhale, ignoring the fleeting wonders of what Noel is like in a relationship. "Fine, fine, all right. Okay. So what is it? You really don't want to kiss me that much?"

"I told you, I never said that," he murmurs, and there's that unusually intense look smouldering in his eyes that threatens to wind me, conjuring tingles from every inch of my body.

I swallow, and silence floods around us.

Against my better judgement, especially with Cleo lounging peacefully in his lap, I take a step forward. Noel's mouth twitches as if he's about to say something, but nothing comes out. The quiet continues, and feeling all the right kinds of dangerous and rebellious, I take another step. Still nothing.

Then I'm hovering right in front of him, crouching down to meet him eye-level, breath hitched in my throat. Noel's still uncharacteristically quiet, eyes burning into mine, the same insatiable curiosity reflected back.

As I lean in, heart thudding two-beats too quick on pure adrenaline alone, the doorbell echoes through the room.

"Oh, come on, are you serious? Is this happening?"

Noel blinks, his face the picture of innocence, and his gaze shifts to the door. "Could you get that? I really don't want to leave Cleopatra alone right now."

I open my mouth to protest, but swallow the words back down, my shoulders sagging in defeat. The world is clearly sending signs and at this point; I need at least five minutes away from everyone to rest and recuperate before even trying to fight it. Instead, I throw my hands up and turn on my heel, retreating to the front door.

It's obviously not Mark- he has keys, after all, and always sends a warning text before making an appearance, which is awfully nice considering it is his own condo, after all. I try to think back if I ordered anything to for delivery, and can't, but food on the other side of this door would not be an unwelcome addition to my life at this point.

Unfortunately, when I pull the door open, there is zero food.

"Cecilia?" I ask, blinking, almost positive that this must be a bizarre dream, maybe nightmare, at this point.

That can be the only reasonable explanation. That, or I'm dead and have finally found hell.

"Vika!" Cecilia gasps in all her nasal-toned glory, a hand glittering with the most obnoxious of rings slapped against her chest and her curled brown hair bouncing with the exaggerated movements. "I've been trying to contact you for like, two weeks!"

I clear my throat, reminded of all the unanswered texts lingering on my phone from an unknown number that I had no intention of making known, and shake my head. "Yeah, uh, my phone. It's, um... broken. Yeah, broken. Haven't gotten any texts. My bad."

The shrug and sheepish grin I give definitely communicates that I was not intentionally ignoring her and hoping that she unexpectedly had to move to Siberia or something. Or even like, Ohio.

Cecilia clicks her tongue, grinning. "Vika," she admonishes, "You're so disconnected, I love it."

She's bounces past me into the living room, leaving me to stand in the doorway, blinking, with the smile still inexplicably frozen on my face.

"What is with rich people and inviting themselves in everywhere?" I murmur under my breath.

"What was that, darling?" Cecilia pauses, throwing a look over her shoulder, a dazzling smile still stretched across her lips.

"Nothing, nothing," I assure her sweetly, slowly clicking the door shut and wondering why it couldn't be pizza on the other side of the door. Pizza wouldn't do this to me. "Uh, what're you here for, Cecilia?"

She turns to me, her mustard yellow dress flouncing about her calves, and pins me with that sly gaze that haunts my darkest nightmares.

"Vika! You've been totally ignoring the Facebook group chat!"

"Yeah, my bad." I shrug, eyes wandering the room.

I may or may not have turned off notifications about 0.02 seconds after being invited.

She laughs. "The bachelorette party, of course! It's next Friday, and we have to iron out all the details! Nat said you weren't working today, and I booked it all off, so we have all day today!" She practically squeals. "I'm so excited!"

I blink.

"All... day?"

She beams. "Yes!"

I wonder what are the chances of Cleo actually killing me if I try to pick her up, but rationalize that even a slow, agonizing, and excruciating death would be better than a day with Cecilia.

Where was that damned demon cat when you need her?

chapter seventeen

THERE HAS TO BE a cut-off level for the amount of karma that can be thrown at one person in a weekly period. And I'm positive I've hit that limit at least three unfortunate events ago.

"I'm sorry, could you repeat that?" I ask, a polite smile frozen on my face.

Nikki stands with her arms crossed over her chest, eyes narrowed and lethal, all-too familiar. "Twenty-one hundred dollars. You owe me twenty-one hundred, and you're going to send it to me. Right now. Don't think I don't know about your little job."

"Job? Never heard of her."

She doesn't laugh, and the scowl engraved on her face deepens. Spiritually, I can feel her murdering me in the most gruesome of ways. It's pretty terrifying, to the point where I hold a palm to my chest, making sure that I'm still alive and in one piece. Which, thankfully, I am.

I can make no promises for five minutes in the future me.

Her crossed arms hare now emphasized with a tap of her shoe, rhythmic and homicidal. I swallow. My gaze falls behind her shoulder and across the hotel room where Nat is innocently sipping a mimosa, pearly sash draped along her body and honey blonde hair cascading down her shoulders. When she meets my eye and then looks to Nikki's 5'4 and somehow still intimidating figure, Nat shoots me a sheepish shrug.

I look back to Nikki, and my nose crinkles. "Okay, okay- you caught me. I have a job now. It's true. Maybe we should cheers?" I lift my mimosa hopefully, but then immediately regret the decision. "No cheers, got it. Money. Okay. Let's talk."

"Did I not make myself clear? Twenty-one hundred dollars."

I nod my head, sucking in a deep breath, the zeros still ringing in my head. "You did throw around that number. I did hear that. Now, let me throw this out there-"

With my mouth open and ready to make some sort of weak defense, I look to her face, and my resolve begins to wilt. Something like a conscious has the feeble excuse of money being tied up at the bank evaporating from my mouth before I can even get it passed my lips. Instead, my shoulders slump.

"Fine," I relent, heaving a tired sigh. "You got me. I'll do it."

"Fine?" Nikki echoes, eyes widening a fraction as her arms fall to her side. "You're actually going to pay me back?"

My brows furrow. "Don't look so surprised, okay? I have some decency." I ignore her lady-like snort while hauling my over-sized faux leather bag onto my lap. "Listen, I don't know who you think you're talking to about twenty-hundred dollars right now-"

"I knew it."

"But," I continue, holding up a hand and preventing any more low-blows to my character from slipping past her mouth, "I'll give you 500, to tide you over, and the rest I'll pay back as soon as I get settled in my new place. You can literally hunt me down for it. I'll even tell you where I live. Or Nat will, because apparently she can't keep her mouth shut about anything."

At her name, the girl of the hour perks up, lifting her glass with a wolfish grin. "If you've got time to talk shit tonight, you've got time to take a shot."

Before I can react, Nikki's stepping into my line of view, arms characteristically folded over her chest as if she's already predicted my response. Her lips thin.

"Now."

I nod, not even thinking to protest, and then begin fishing my phone from my purse. Nikki's hawk-like gaze is unwavering as my thumbs brush along the glass screen, and with a heavy heart, I show her the confirmation of the e-transfer as soon as the deed is done.

She takes a moment to drink it in, eyes narrowing in doubt, before she nods. "Don't think I'm letting you off the hook for the rest."

Then Nikki's sweeping over to the opposite side of the room, to a table meticulously arranged with pastel pink napkins, an overflowing charcuterie board, and a bag of Cheetos that were my very significant addition.

The hotel, the dinner, the smoked extra-aged cheddar and foie gras were all charged to Cecilia's credit card, with my helpful additions being my patience, my time, and my Cheetos. There wasn't much I could do anyway, considering that she'd already had a binder, colour-coded and highlighted to the nines that cared little about what I thought about bachelorette party etiquette.

"I'm so glad I invited you, Nikki! Isn't it fun that everyone could make it?" Cecilia beams, wearing the same broad grin that's been stitched onto her face since the night has started. "You guys are seriously too funny."

I shrug. "I mean, what's funnier than living in the fiery pits of debt, am I right?"

Nat arches a brow at me with a small smirk, a look I know will be the first of many tonight, but Cecilia in all Cecilia-fashion lets it roll off her shoulder like nothing. She laughs, a voice like wind-chimes in a hurricane, and I throw her back an empty smile that I've practiced to an unnatural degree for the past week.

I'm honestly surprised Nat hasn't bestowed me with a trophy for not murdering, maiming, or even emotionally destroying Cecilia through our time together. Even if it got pretty close when she wouldn't stop harassing me about the essential difference between ballet-slipper and baby pink napkins that would completely decide our bachelorette party fate.

We went with ballet-slipper.

I think.

I was clearly more concerned with the tiny-penis shot glasses and getting bottle service at the strip-club. I had more important things on my mind.

"Okay, so we have dinner here at 8, and then we're going to come back up here for a couple fun bachelorette games," her voice lowers as if she's talking about something sultry or devious, when she is, in fact, talking about "sexy" scrapbooking and charades, "and then I think Vika has something planned."

Nat catches my eye.

"Spoiler alert, it's various half-naked men gyrating with their crotch in your face."

Nat bursts out laughing, along with our mutual university friend Christina who's next to her, and some of Nat's work friends that have also made an appearance. Cecilia's very polite, shooting me a smile that I think she thinks means we've bonded, but at least Nikki even cracks a grin.

"Okay, okay, let's all have a celebratory drink to get this night started!" Cecilia chimes, clapping her hands together, and it's the first idea she's ever had that I'm in complete agreement with.

Cecilia and Nat's co-workers all have a mimosa in hand, but I am quick to shove a penis-shaped shot glass of tequila at Nat, which Nikki also joins in on. As we stand in a circle in the middle of the hotel room that I don't even want to imagine the fee of, I meet Nat's gaze in the middle, and we share a smile as we clink glasses and throw back Jose Cuervo, the first of many.

In fact, it's tequila and tequila alone that gets me through the duck liver dinner, which turns out a lot better than expected, and then the ever-excruciating scrapbooking portion of the night. The number of small dicks I draw on just about anything rivals that of a fifth-grade boy and has me banned from all markers, pencils, or other marking utensils. Luckily for myself, Nat is matching me shot for shot, so it isn't too far into the night until I'm allowed to steal the reigns from Cecilia, who, admittedly I'm softening my position on after she may or may not have made a sucking dick joke.

Jury's still out, but I'm hopeful.

"And another one!" I cheer, tapping my shot glass against Nat's, who's already got a faint flush dusting her cheeks.

Surprisingly, Cecilia joins in, and I fondly look over to see she's holding a tiny penis in hand. A ballet-slipper pink tiny penis.

And then the night brings us to my venue of choice, The Fox's Den, that has all the gyrating and hip swinging and pants ripping that I've promised. Nat's virginal-white sash calls to the dancers like a beacon, and I almost shred my vocal chords cheering when she's dragged on stage and pushed onto a chair, her eyes wide but appreciative of all the things that are currently happening right in front of her face.

Cecilia even gives a whoop-whoop of her own.

It's when I'm casually sipping on a tequila sunrise, a pleasant buzz humming under my skin and a looseness to all my limbs, that I notice that Nat's disappeared for a moment. Within the darkness, interrupted only by the colourful lights that are spitting out from the DJ booth, her blonde head of hair is nowhere to be seen.

I pause mid-conversation with Christina, who I think I'm pretty successfully convincing that I'm just as stable as with her five-year relationship and newly bound engagement, and search the room. Cecilia has let her dark hair loose from the constrains of a high-ponytail and is eyeing the dancer on stage with approving eyes, and the rest of Nat's co-workers are talking amongst themselves. The girl in question is nowhere in sight.

"I'll be right back, gotta go find Nat," I tell Christina and she nods, taking a sip of her drink and turning back to the stage.

As I meander my way out through the door to outside, I'm greeted by the familiar noise of the city's nightlife. It's only a few moments of confused glances thrown here and there before the bouncer points me around the corner. Under the yellow wash of light from a lamp in the alleyway, I find Nat crouched on a step, attention directed to the phone in her hand. Thankfully, she still has her strappy black heels on.

"If that's Mark on the other end, I swear to god Nat, I'm going to football tackle you right in this murder alley."

Her head shoots up, and she grins. "We both know I'm faster than you."

I scoff, dropping down on the stoop next to her, a faint breeze whispering past my bare arms. The oncoming summer is already in the air, though, and the warmth blossoming from the tequila inside is enough to keep me from caring too much.

"How is his phone also not confiscated? When did you even steal that from my purse? I thought I had your phone on lock. I'm calling to yell at Noel for being an awful best man," I say, bumping my shoulder into her's and unsurprised when I see Mark's name written at the top of her phone screen.

Still, it gives me a distraction from the tingle that shoots down my spine at Noel's name in my mouth.

"It's just a simple text!" she defends herself, the slight slur of Cuervo on her tongue. "I'm just curious what they're up to, is all. Is that so bad?"

Her green eyes are so drunkenly hopeful, it's cute.

"Yes," I answer. "It's all the bad. Come on, you'll both be home tonight, stop canoodling. Tonight is not about canoodling, it's about seeing naked people dance for money and getting unquestionably wasted. What is that, did he text back? No, give it to me," I demand, quickly shooting out my hand to steal her phone away, and she's two seconds too late before she realizes it's gone.

Somewhere along the night I'd slowed down in the shots department in the hopes of being at least semi-responsible for Nat, in return for all the nights where the roles were reversed, and I'm actually much quicker than her. She gasps, eyes wide, but then leans her body against mine.

"Is it bad that I'm excited?"

I arch a brow. "For the extra-large pizza each we're both going to stuff our faces with later? Why would it be bad? It's ninety percent of what I'm looking forward to tonight."

She giggles, shaking her head. "No, no, I mean about Mark."

"Listen, if he wants pizza, he's going to have to get his own, I'm not about this sharing business-"

"No, stupid," she cuts me off, snorting. "I mean, we're out tonight, but I'm still excited to go home later because I know he'll be there."

There's a dumb grin plastered across her face, all pearly whites as she stares off down the alleyway, something like a wistful sigh threading through her exhale.

My nose crinkles. "Fine- fine, just rub it in my face how much you hate this bachelorette party that not only I but Cecilia also poured our heart and goddamn souls into, Nat. Just shit all over it."

When I meet her eye, I can't stop myself from bursting out laughing.

"Shut up, you know tonight was perfect. Is perfect. You actually killed it, Vika," she murmurs, resting her head on my shoulder, voice barely breaking above the hum of the city.

"I didn't really do anything- seriously. The cheese platters and the dinner, that was all Cecilia. I will take credit for all the various penis-themed merchandise, oh, and the Cheetos. But that's about it. Cecilia actually killed it," I admit, a tad begrudgingly, staring up into the night sky.

"But the shot glasses were everything."

"Right?" I gasp. "I knew it, thank you. I don't know why Cecilia was so against them, they were basically the highlight of this entire night."

"And you didn't get blackout drunk. Look at you, being able to walk and talk and whatnot," Nat says, linking her arm with mine with a small chuckle.

"I'm a regular Mother Teresa, you know me."

Nat lifts her head and when I turn my gaze to meet hers, they're uncharacteristically soft. She smiles, eyes falling shut. "Thanks, Vika. For tonight, for everything."

"Save the praise for when I get you safely home all in one piece. There's still a good chunk of the night left, and my opportunities to fuck up are endless. Have you met me?" I roll my eyes and disentangle our arms, lifting to my feet.

She beams, accepting my outstretched hand and pulling herself up. "I thought having a total stranger as my maid of honour would be so kitschy, don't you think?"

I laugh and then we're stumbling back through the doors, the bass of a techno song thumping in our ears and a hazy film over our eyes either from the low lighting or the tequila shots. Just as I drop Nat's phone in my purse, zipping it up with a pointed look in the girl's direction, I come to another unfortunate realization that Cecilia is now pulling the disappearing act.

Asking some of the girls if they've seen her prove little results, until Christina, bless her heart, mentions something about Cecilia and the bathroom. Nat moves to get up, but I stop her with a hand and instead shove another shot in her direction, which, as expected, completely distracts her.

My maid of honour duty is in full throttle.

Down the steps with the directions of a scantily dressed bronze and beautiful man, I eventually find the bathroom. The little lady on the sign doesn't lead me astray as I push open the door, the harsh fluorescent lights greeting me along with the very poignant stench of cleaner.

"Cecilia?" I call out, peering into one of the bathroom stalls.

"Here," someone croaks, which seems like Cecilia in context but does not sound like her at all. "I'm in the last stall."

Brows furrowed, I trek over to the other side, thankful that it seems we're the only ones in here. Just as I step in front of the chipping grey metal door, it swings open, and I sigh.

"Well, fuck."

chapter eighteen

"OH, HI VIKA."

I pause, needing a moment to drink in the scene that's in front of me. Her navy-blue cocktail dress is pooling around her thighs, back pressed against the stall's metal wall, head lolling onto her shoulder. Barely processing my presence is her watery blue-green eyes, an echo of Mark's. I don't need to take a glance inside the rim of the porcelain throne to know why she's found solace in the bathroom.

I never figured I'd be the one on the other side.

"Hey, Cecilia. What's up? How you feeling, girl?" I ask, baring my teeth in more of a grimace than a smile.

Her brows knit with a quiet intensity, a strand of dark hair falling between her eyes. Her lips part to answer, and it seems we both realize at the same time that something a little more than words is going to spill out as she instantly swerves her head in the toilet's direction.

I wince as she collapses into a fit of coughs and drops to a crouch. The sound of splashing water makes my nose crinkle. Seeing her hair dangerously close to the seat of the toilet, I sweep it away from her face, but she doesn't seem to notice.

"You still have that hair tie?" I ask with a sympathetic frown.

She nods, but doesn't say anything, only reaching behind to give me access to the black band clinging to her wrist. I gently tug it off and pull her hair back into a looser ponytail than she'd had this morning. I think I hear a mumble of thanks, but then she's disintegrating into a round of dry heaves that have empathy tickling in the back of my throat.

"Just get it out, seriously. You'll feel so much better when you get it all out," I say, rubbing a comforting hand up and down her back, surprising myself with the tender notes in my voice.

She nods again and is all too-quick to take my advice. I draw a deep breath and continue running my fingers along her spine, reaching to tug her dress down a bit, not that it seems like anyone else will join us. Still, as much as I'd pictured her face getting run over by an 18-wheeler many a time, the pathetic little garbles she's making has me wanting to make this as painless as possible.

Hopefully, I can find a permanent mailing address for them to send my Nobel Peace Prize sometime soon.

"I'm not- this is so not like me," Cecilia says once she's finally caught her breath again. "I'm so sorry. I didn't mean-"

I throw up a hand to cut her off. "Oh my god- hey, stop, listen to me. Stop that, you're fine. I am the last person you need to be explaining yourself to. As least you got it into the toilet- I have done so much worse."

She lifts her chin, palm slapped over her forehead and a frown marked on her face, apparently not comforted by my lack of human decency. "This is so not like me."

I raise my brows, unable to tell who she's trying to convince more.

"Trust me when I say this is the most I've liked you since I met you. And I truly mean that."

Her brows pinch in confusion, and I snort, trying and failing to restrain my grin. There's mascara smudged under her eyes and a washed-out quality to her face that makes it look like I'm staring into a mirror of my twenty-two-year-old self, or really, my self probably six months ago. It looks as if she's about to argue, but a precarious burp bubbles up her throat and she takes a pause.

"Listen, take your time. Nat's pretty preoccupied upstairs, and the club doesn't close for another hour or so. It doesn't look like anyone's coming down here, either," I reassure her, giving her a small pat on the arm.

"Does that mean you like me?" Cecilia asks, finally, and there's a weak smile on her face.

I roll my eyes. "I know you're drunk, but I don't think you're delusional."

"You like me. You're- you're starting to like me. I feel it."

She meets my gaze in a challenge, small burps of pure tequila breaking through her grin. I heave a sigh.

"I still do not care about what colour the napkins are or how old the cheese is, for any occasion ever, but seeing that you're an actual human being and not a robot is making me warm up to you. Slightly. Stop smiling. I'm taking it back."

"You like me!" she beams, and she throws her arms out, to which I immediately back away. "C'mon," she interrupts herself with a hiccup, "Let's hug this out!"

I gesture to the toilet between us with a frown. "Cute sentiment, let's not forget why we're here though."

She pauses, then drops her arms. "That's fair," she admits, nodding her head, but the grin is still lingering on her face. "Glad we did this though."

"We should probably focus more on getting out of here alive before we pat ourselves on the back."

"So, this was fun?" she asks, ignoring me, head falling back to press against the metal stall. "It was fun, wasn't it? I hope so, at least. I've been looking forward to this for months."

There's a bite back that almost instinctively rolls off my tongue, but I stop myself when I see her. There's something genuine in her eyes that I can't find it in me to squander. "It was fun. This is fun. Maybe a little too much fun for you, though." I arch a brow. "You've been downing shots like a champion tonight."

Her eyes slowly fall to a close, on purpose or unconsciously I'm not sure, and she grins. "Fun. It's been fun."

Silence falls over us, and I tug down her dress a little more again, the unconscious action I don't realize until I've already done it. Her chest is rising and falling with her small breaths, which reassures me she's still alive, thankfully, despite her otherwise lack of movement. When a few more moments pass of nothing, though, my brows knit.

"Hey!" I snap my fingers in front of her face, to which she barely acknowledges with only a flutter of her lashes. "No sleeping! Stop! We're staying awake here!"

She blindly swats my hands away, groaning, eyes still defiantly shut.

"Fine," I surrender with a tired sigh, lifting to my feet. "I'll be back in two seconds, don't go anywhere."

She mumbles something incoherent in acknowledgement as I rip off a chunk of toilet paper and push open the door, but it's not worth even trying to decipher. When I'm running cold water over the paper, I think I hear some more unintelligible grumbles, but figure she's still trying to convince me the severe importance of sending out invitation cards in the mail.

"Cecilia, seriously, I don't think anyone but you cares that much about making scrapbook memories," I say, my sentence falling short as I push open the door to find that she is not as I'd left her.

She looks up through half-lidded eyes, still glazed over with the hazy film of alcohol, but her mouth keeps moving. "Yeah, come get me." She's pressing her phone to her ear. "Now. Thanks. Yes."

I frown. "Who's that?"

She doesn't immediately answer me. I assume the conversation is over as her phone slips from her grasp, clanging against the tile floor, and she meets my eye. "They're coming."

"Well, that's not ominous at all," I murmur, brows raised as I drop to a crouch. "And who would they be?"

She accepts my wet toilet paper offer and sets it on her forehead, eyes falling closed again, a relieved sigh spilling from her lips. "This is nice. You're being so nice. I like this."

"Cecilia," I say, voice a little stronger. "Who was that? Help me, help you. Did you call the government to pick you up because you're glitching? Are these aliens coming to take you and Noel home? Give me something to work with."

"Listen, shh, it's gonna be okay. They said they're coming."

She's not lying, as that's exactly what 'they' end up doing. They are made up of Mark's bachelor party, including the man himself, Cecilia's husband, and Noel trailing along after them with the worst Best Man presence I've ever seen. I've dragged Cecilia up from the downstairs bathroom onto the street in one piece, mostly with some semblance of coherence, and am all too ready to pass her off to the broad-shouldered man she practically flings herself at.

"Remember, liquids, it's all about the liquids," I say, mostly to her husband who's gently maneuvering her with a Herculean amount of patience into the taxicab. He shoots me an understanding smile and I'm comforted I'm at least leaving her in good hands. "Get lots of sleep."

Cecilia sticks her head out of the cab and points a finger at me. "The fish! Don't forget the fish!"

"Yes, yes, the fish. Don't worry Cecilia, the fish will be okay," I reassure her like a child, not even trying to follow her deranged thought process at this point, and wave her goodbye. "Sleep tight."

The touch of relaxation that spreads through my muscles is short-lived as I watch her taxi disappear down the road, only to be to cut short by a pair of arms locking around me. Hot breath fans across my neck.

"Who are you and what have you done with my best friend?"

I roll my eyes as Nat giggles in my ear, turning in her hold to be met with the heart-shaped face and round green eyes of my best friend, bathed in the glow of the streetlights. Only a few steps behind is Mark, with his tie loosened around his neck and a telltale flush of scotch on his face, throwing me a half-coherent wave.

"Do not get used this. You will be scraping my body off the pavement in no time once that ring is glued to your finger," I say, holding her at an arm's length and shooting her a pointed look.

She beams, laughing, and captures me into a tight hug. "Thank you."

When she pulls away, Nat can no longer resist Mark's gravitational pull, and surrenders back to his side. They're both grinning so hard I wonder if their faces might break, and another cab pulls up to the curb.

"Thanks mom!" Nat calls out before ducking into the backseat, flailing her arms wildly in goodbye.

I snort. "Get out of here before I throw up, seriously."

Mark gives me a drunken salute and also tucks himself into the cab, both of them driving into the distance. I'm left holding my arms on the sidewalk, the 2AM crowd thinning and a touch of fatigue pulling a yawn from my lips. There's still the haze of a buzz, but playing parent has fought back most of it. Still, when I wave my arms, trying to hail my own cab, it takes me a moment to register the tap on my shoulder.

"Surprised that you're still able to walk," comes the soft voice with an edge of condescension that I'm all too familiar with, right behind my shoulder.

"I'm sorry, were you named parent of the evening? No, because I'm the only one that earned it."

When I twirl around, it's the first time we've been toe-to-toe, eye-to-eye, since we'd been interrupted by the converging forces of Cleopatra and Cecilia who seemed hell-bent on keeping my chastity under lock. I can't help the hitch in my throat as my gaze drifts from the small smile on his face to the darkness of his eyes, realizing that both those forces have disappeared.

My pulse trips as he leans closer, our gazes fusing in the midnight air. His smile manifests into a smirk. We're dangerously close.

Only for him to completely slip by me.

I make a small noise of indignation as I pivot on my heel, watching as he ever-so nonchalantly climbs into the cab that I'd hailed and was too distracted to notice.

"Hey!" I protest. "Dude, that's my cab!"

The door's still open, and I watch as he shifts to the farther seat, a cool smile tugging on the corner his mouth. He gestures to the empty space. "You're welcome to join me."

We lock eyes.

As another breeze whistles passed, teeming with the low hum of the city. I pause. I can see an oncoming cab down the road, presenting itself as an option, but when I'm drawn back to those dark brown eyes, I'm already following in after him.

The tequila on my tongue is fueled by the nerves igniting inside of me, pressed next to him in the backseat, and I shift.

"I'm not paying," I mumble, crossing my arms over my chest and staring aggressively out the window. "This is going on your tab."

"It didn't even cross my mind," he says, and the genuine notes in his voice threaten to disarm me completely. "Davenport and Bay, thanks."

This is directed to the driver who gives a nod of confirmation before pulling back into oncoming traffic. My brows knit.

"That's not Mark's," I say, unsure of where I'm going with it.

"It's my place, but we can make a detour, if you want. I can drop you off, it's on my tab after all."

I turn my head, caught off guard to find that he's already looking to me. My fingers grip tighter to my phone, settled in my sweaty palm. Despite all the buildup to this moment, all the pent-up frustrations and clandestine glances, the realization is crashing into me all at once. I swallow.

"We wouldn't want to waste this nice man's time," I say, nodding to the driver. Noel grins.

The rest of the trip to Noel's place is filled with small talk about the night, slightly slurred words that have no consequence to the warmth of his body next to mine, the promise of heat in the night to come. In the lulls of conversation, my gaze falls out the window and my imagination spins fervently at the thought of Noel's home.

When the cab pulls to a stop, and Noel hands over a few bills, I'm both shocked and not at all to step out in front of the looming, thirty storey building that is a Carlton hotel. It's all gleaming glass and stainless steel, overshadowing the both of us as we walk towards the entrance. Inside is no touch less luxurious, with a glittering chandelier imposing in the middle of the room, bathing the tan and sandalwood interior with its soft light. I feel more like an intruder than a guest as I follow quickly after Noel, who nods at the receptionist as if it's nothing.

We're the only ones in the lobby, and I'm hovering a little more close than comfort when we find the elevator doors.

"Hey," I murmur softly, bumping his shoulder with mine. "Don't get any weird ideas. If you think you're going to get me into this elevator and suddenly, I won't be able to control myself or something, you're wrong."

The doors resound with a ding and slowly pull open. Noel looks down to me, the corner of his mouth turned up. "I would never assume such things." He gestures to the space. "Ladies first."

I fix him with a sharp look and step inside, making a pointed effort to tuck myself into the corner. He follows, still wearing that infuriating smile, and the doors slowly pull closed.

When the elevator dings open, my dress is pulled up to my belly button.

"Noel, Noel, door," I gasp, pushing him off me and tugging my dress down, thankful that the hallway is similarly deserted as the lobby after two in the morning. "The door's open."

He peels himself off me with a small "fuck" that resounds all the way into my bones. As my body is lamenting the lack of physical contact, he slips his hand in mine and tugs me along in a way that's more personal that we've ever touched before. I blink and blindly follow.

We reach a door that Noel pauses at, and with a swipe of a card we're in. Noel's house is surprisingly exactly as I'd imagined, cold and clean to an almost clinical precision. He flips on a light, illuminating the rooms to his suite, and there's not one speck of dust out of place. Shoes lined properly in the closet, a potted plant tucked in the corner, the glass and stainless steel motif of the entire hotel echoed in all I can see.

The warmth of his palm is still nestled in mine as he tugs me into the bedroom.

I barely have time to process it before he's closing the door and pressing me up against it with his lips on mine, hands suddenly all over my skin all at once.

"Wait," I pause, pulling away, catching my breath. He suspends his assault on my neck, to both my pleasure and dismay. "I want to be on the same page here. No cat?"

When he lifts his chin and meets my gaze, those familiar pupils blown wide in a way that makes my pulse stutter, he nods. "No cat." A crooked grin stretched across his face.

"All right, awesome, no cat. Thank god, you've been such a tease," I beam, toying with the hair tickling the nape of his neck.

"Tease?" he murmurs, returning his lips to pepper gentle kisses down my jawline. "Have you seen the dress you're wearing today?"

I grin. "How kind of you to notice."

His fingers travel down to play with the edge of my black, tight-fitting dress, lifting the fabric up my thighs, belly button, and then finally over my head. I'm thankful that I had an inkling of one of us making a move tonight, and I'm wearing a matching pearlescent lace set that I spent way too much money on, but seems to be paying off in the best kind of way as he takes a step back.

I'm unsurprised as his eyes immediately gravitate towards my chest. His wandering gaze leaves a trail of fire in its wake, scorching into my skin in the most delightful kind of way. I'm half-mesmerized by the dip of his Adam's apple in his throat.

"Are you going to do something or just stare?"

When I arch a brow, Noel looks up, meeting my gaze. Unconsciously or not, his tongue runs along his top lip. I swallow, and he smiles, takes a step forward, just breaths between us.

"We've got all the time in the world, Vika."

And somehow, staring into those coffee dark eyes, I believe him.

chapter nineteen

"I TOTALLY GET IT NOW, you're right, these are amazing."

Noel looks up from behind his thick frames, a coffee hovering just below his lips and his dark hair still tousled with sleep. It's the first time he's torn his gaze from his phone screen since he'd sat on the couch twenty minutes ago, despite all my very convincing calls for him to come back to bed.

He tilts his head. "Are you wearing my boxers?"

I beam and continue strutting around the room, the silken black boxers I'd pulled from the bedroom floor brushing against my bare thighs. I'd considered going for the entire ensemble and grabbing his dress shirt to finish the outfit, but figured I'd more likely catch his attention with more skin than less, and swiped up my bra from the floor instead.

And judging by the way his eyes linger, it works.

I grin. "I mean, they're still super pretentious, don't get me wrong. But I also feel like a high-power CEO in these things. Get my faxes! Karen, make me an appointment! Tell the queen I must reschedule!"

A small smile curves on his face, lighting up all the way to his eyes. "I'm not a CEO, that's my uncle, remember? I do get to sit on the board, though."

I stop in my tracks, frowning. "Shit, really? Damn, bamboozled again. Could you be a darling and pass along his number to me, then?"

When his face immediately falls, I'm laughing. He smooths out his brows with a dry look, and I take this moment of distraction to cross the room and gently steal away his coffee cup, still chuckling. I'm surprised with how easily he lets me.

Instead, he arches his brow. "You know, I said I could make you a cup. You don't have to take mine."

I nod, taking a small sip before setting it down on the tempered glass and stainless steel end table. Noel is quick to lean over and slide a coaster underneath the mug, to which I roll my eyes. Still, I'm undeterred as I steal his divided attention and crawl into his lap, each leg on either side, caging him in underneath me. He's wearing just a soft cotton t-shirt and sweatpants, a side of him that excites me more than any pressed Armani suit, leaving little layers between the two of us.

"You know when a lady calls for you to come back to bed, you should listen to her," I say, reaching to grab his phone with little resistance on his part.

"Where's the lady here?"

"Noel!" I gasp, slapping his chest with the back of my hand. "Is this what you do? Trick girls into bed with you and then be mean to them?"

He tilts his head back. "Wasn't it you who tried to drunkenly grope me from the beginning?"

"Looks like it worked, so whatever." I shrug my shoulders.

His reply is only a muted smile, and a dip of his gaze from my eyes to my cupid's bow, communicating more than words ever could. I take his face in my palms and pull him close to me, already missing the warmth of his mouth on mine despite the night's worth of kisses we'd already shared. His lips are soft and familiar in an oddly comforting way, moving against mine with a natural sense of style that's too easy to get lost in.

Meaning, I'm surprised when he pulls away, eyes wide. "Cleopatra."

I crinkle my nose. "Listen, I'm a pretty open-minded person, but I don't think this is the type of roleplay I can get behind."

His eyes immediately re-calibrate into a deadpan. "If we're both here, there's no one to feed Cleopatra. We have to go back to Mark's."

"Isn't she smart enough to feed herself? Isn't that why you bought one of those fancy leopard cats in the first place?"

My response is him gently but still forcefully nudging me off his lap, letting me fall into the couch as he lifts to his feet. I pout, grabbing at the air and whining for him to come back, my skin already feeling too cold without his pressed against it, but he doesn't pay any mind to any of it, unfortunately. Instead, he throws me a look over his shoulder.

"Get dressed, I'm going to call a cab."

I shoot him a dry stare, but all he returns it with is a small smile that too endearing for his own good. It leaves little room for argument, though, even more so when he steps out of his room in a familiar pants and dress shirt combo that objectively looks good but is the exact opposite of what I want to see him in. With little choice and many loud and insistent complaints, I drag myself to a stand and sweep my little black dress off the floor, much less appealing in the morning light.

"Do you need clothes?" Noel asks, pausing in the doorway.

I'm still in the middle of the room, holding out the dress in front of me. "I know that I'd be super hot in your dress shirt and boxers, but we are going outside, Noel. Control yourself."

He scoffs, the edge of his mouth digging into his cheek. "My sister has clothes here- I'm sure you could fit into them."

I'm oddly surprised by this, even more so when he leads me to another room with a cream-coloured wardrobe tucked in the corner. When I pull open some drawers, I almost feel like an intruder to find an entire closet's worth tucked inside, from blouses to socks to more intimates. Noel doesn't seem to think anything of it as he toys with the cuff of his dress shirt behind me.

I pull out a pair of jeans with a frown. "Are these child's sizes?"

"She's got more than just jeans in there. You'll be fine. If you want, I can help you squeeze into them." His dark eyes flash.

I snort. "You've clearly never tried to fit your ass in skinny jeans before, there's probably nothing less sexy in the world other than a whale giving birth."

He laughs, and I return to rifling through the rest of the clothes, managing to find something that fits like she'd at least bought it from the adult's section- a tasteful pair of black trousers with gilded gold buttons. The fabric is soft under my fingertips, and when I take a glimpse at the tag inside, I parch.

"These are Cavalli," I choke out, eyes the size of saucers.

Noel tilts his head. "And?"

"These," I say, turning to him and holding up the pants. "These are rent. Probably rent times two, honestly."

"It's fine," he reassures me, dismissing my worries with a wave of his hand. "If anything, I'll just get her another pair. Don't worry about it, just put them on. Cleopatra's waiting."

I'm holding them as if someone has set a newborn child in my arms, drinking in every stitch in complete awe. The numbers are still ringing in my head as I slip them on, snug around me in the most luxurious of ways. When I stare at myself in the floor-length mirror, I feel as if I'm only two seconds away from getting football tackled by some beefy security man.

Something inside of me involuntarily warms, though, when he throws a pullover of his in my direction, smelling of fresh linen and sharp citrus. I have to hide my smile when I throw it on and grab my purse.

"So do I get like a goodie bag or something?" I ask when we step out of the elevator doors and into the soft cream and white oak of the lobby. "Some autographs, some jewelry? Anything that'll save me from eviction on eBay?"

Noel fixes me with a measured stare. "I'm not a baseball player. I don't think people care who I am unless they have a subscription to Forbes or Business Insider."

I cock a brow. "This sweater?"

"I like that sweater," he says, frowning.

"Not even for your favourite hooker?"

He shoots me a look.

I roll my eyes and laugh, pushing open the hotel doors and immediately greeted with the spring breeze, alive with the overflowing hum of the city. It's nice on my bare skin, the warmth a reminder of the summer only days away. It almost all dawns at me at once, how much time has passed, since Nat had first barged through my door with that glittering rock on her ring finger, to looking up in Mark's doorway to find that there wasn't a pizza delivery guy on the other side, but a man in a sharp suit with cold eyes instead. I can't help the small smile on my face as I watch him pull open the cab door, gesturing for me to go inside.

"Don't think I'm taking that ten thousand dollars off the table because you're opening some doors for me," I beam before tucking myself in the backseat.

Noel follows after me, and we settle a respectable distance away from each other, to both my understanding and dismay. It's only a minute into the car ride when his phone lights up, vibrating in his palm and capturing both of our attention.

Surprisingly, he lets the call die without answering.

"Important?" I ask, catching his eye.

"Work."

I pause, searching his face but finding nothing, an echo of when we first met, lips thin and eyes cool.

"On a Sunday?"

There's a small, heartless smile that slips on his face. "Hotels don't stop running on the weekend, unfortunately."

"What kind of work weeks are you pulling?" My eyes widen. "Shit, I complain when Marissa shows up late for her shift and I have to stay an extra hour."

His face is guarded in ways that I feel as whispers on the back of my neck. "That's why Mark got me Cleopatra- cats are nocturnal, after all."

"Why is she at Mark's then? Why don't you have her at your place?" The curiosity asks for me, before I realize my mouth is forming around the words.

"My sister- she doesn't like cats, and she's been staying with me the last couple of months. Problems with her husband," he explains, gazing back down to his phone that is already lit up with another call. "That's why Cleopatra has to stay at Mark's, hopefully not for much longer. Angelica doesn't like to be alone, but she's also stubborn as fuck."

There's a vulnerability that's so fresh on his face I want to kiss it. Instead, I offer him a half-smile.

"Runs in the family?"

There's a little more heart in the next smile that he shoots me.

The drive from Noel's to Mark's isn't too long, and he's still pretty absorbed in his phone when we pull up, which I don't mind too much. Every time he heaves a sigh, the bags under his eyes grow a little darker, but they're not as bad as they usually are. He's so consumed with the screen that he doesn't even realize that we've parked next to the curb of Mark's condo until I've already climbed out, trekked to the other side, and pulled open the door.

His eyes are wide when he peers up.

"We've arrived, Sir Carlton. Would you like me to grab your luggage? Can I interest you in a cappuccino? On the house, of course."

He rolls his eyes, passing over some bills to the driver before following out after me and back up into Mark's apartment.

Despite the neon coloured sticky notes that are dotting several surfaces of the apartment with various addresses scrawled on them of apartments up for rent, courtesy of Nat, there's still a home-like quality that greets me when I step inside. My sweater is hung up on the back of one of the chairs, a glass I'd left out still sitting on the countertop. I quickly swipe up one of the sticky notes from the cupboard as I grab a mug.

"Do you want water?" I ask, throwing a look over my shoulder to see Noel searching in the living room.

"I'm okay," Noel says, brows pinched. "Is Cleopatra in there?"

My eyes graze the tile floor, to the empty food bowl and water, finding no traces of the cat. "Nope! Which is weird, she's usually bounding up to me and declaring her undying love the moment I step through the door. Wonder what's up with her today."

When I meander my way into the living room, I find Noel crouched on the ground, peering underneath the couch. That characteristic frown is etched on his face.

"Can you help me look?"

I hum, taking a sip from my water. "What's in it for me?"

"You get to keep the pants."

I instantly perk up. "We're going on a cat hunt. Gonna catch a moody one!"

We finally find Cleo in the guest bedroom- a room she barely ventures into, probably feeling my presence in these four walls even when I'm not around, and preferring to not be tainted by my peasant aura. I see her distinctive striped tail first, the black tip followed by the golden brown, and then step inside to see the rest of her. Her green eyes barely acknowledge my presence, though, and return at lightning speeds back to the new addition that's sitting on my dresser.

I pause, blinking, frozen in the doorway. "What is that?"

Noel brushes passed me, immediately reaching to scoop Cleo up in his arms until he realizes that even he barely warrants more than a passing glance from the cat. I watch as he follows her fierce and unwavering gaze to the dresser.

"You have a fish?" he asks, turning to me with confusion reflected in his dark eyes.

I shake my head. "I do not have a fish."

He reaches for a note that's sitting next to a small bowl where a burst of red and purple is swimming around idly, and he scans what's written. "Seems like it's a bachelorette party gift from Cecilia?" he hazards, a frown tugging down his lips.

Something inside of me tightens. "What that seems like is a responsibility."

"Were we supposed to give out gifts? I mean, I got cigars for every one..."

"I have to feed it every day?" I ask to no one in particular, wincing at the thought. "Like every day?"

Noel's scratching his jaw. "Would a cigar cover the gifts? I'm not sure, Mark didn't say anything about gifts, and I've never really done this before."

"I'm seriously going to be sent to fish hell if I kill another one of these guys." I'm pulling at the skin of my cheeks now. "I cannot go to fish hell, there's so many other kinds of hell that I'm already going to be going to."

"I should've asked Angelica on the etiquette for this kind of thing, she must know, I mean, she does this kind of thing all the time. It's basically her job. Why didn't I ask her?"

"Focus, Noel!" I snap, shaking my hands and causing him to pause with his mouth open mid-thought. "We've got bigger problems here than fucking etiquette!"

He blinks. "Actually, the fish is very small."

"Oh my god," I groan, unable to ignore the way that the dread is pooling at the base of my stomach. "I am filled with so much regret right now."

Which is true, for some reason that splash of indigo has my insides gnawing anxiously on themselves, something uncharacteristic forming in my throat. Even though this fish clearly doesn't give much thought to either of us standing here, or the cat staring at it with murder in her green eyes, it's somehow dredging up more than just the worry of a responsibility from the dark chambers inside of me. I swallow, hard.

With my hair still mussed from Noel's hands, and my legs firmly wrapped in a pair of pants I had no business even touching, standing in a condo that was never supposed to be mine, there're whispers of fraud in my ear.

"Why are you getting so upset over this? It's just a fish," Noel says, brows raised in my direction.

There's still hungover tequila lingering in the back of my throat, and I have to pause at the way the filtered sunlight pours in from the window, catching the Rolex on his wrist and the frames of his glasses.

"It's not just a fish, Noel," I insist, something harsh in the undertones of my voice.

His phone vibrates, and he checks it, again. "Just feed it," he murmurs, as if were the most obvious thing in the world. "You'll be fine, it's not rocket science by any means."

My jaw instinctively clenches at the dismissive tone in his voice. "Well, isn't that just so easy for you to say. I'm Noel, I can just pay someone to talk care of ten thousand fish because I have so much money and therefore I'm better than everyone."

The words are spilling out before I can stop them, and they hang in the air, wrapped up in a bitterness that's still lingering on my tongue. I can't find it in myself to take them back, and so I don't. Acid reflux is licking up my throat. Every sane voice inside of me is demanding that I avert my eyes, anywhere but his face, but I can't.

Noel pauses, taken aback, and meets my eye. Stone replaces all his features, gaze narrowed in a way that's scorching into me. "Vika, it's a fucking fish. Anyone can keep a fish alive."

There's a beat of quiet between us, my nerves still igniting under my skin and a nausea flooding in my stomach. I swallow.

"You're right," I concede, voice tight. "It's a fucking fish. You're right."

Despite my words, Noel visibly deflates, the coldness of his face evaporating to reveal a concern that doesn't comfort me at all. "Wait, that's not- I didn't mean it like that."

"It's fine," I reassure him, my words still small. "It's- whatever. I'll see you later. Don't worry about it."

His brows furrow. "Where are you going? This is your place."

I pause in the doorway, drawing a deep breath, burdened by the newfound weight pressing against my chest. The words are stale, hiding behind my teeth all this time, and they taste bitter in my mouth.

"Noel, we both know this place was never mine."

chapter twenty

THE ONLY PROBLEM with storming out of your own house for dramatic effect is that afterward you can't go back, and you have to go somewhere, but sometimes you can't justify the third Starbucks drink of the week when you still owe your cousin sixteen hundred dollars.

Which leaves little options of where to go next, especially when I have like three friends, and honestly, Nat's the only one I actually like. And that leaves me knocking on her door, still wrapped up in Noel's hoodie that smells too much like the man himself to be any sort of comfort against the spring air. There's a lingering knot tight in my throat when the door is pulled open to reveal the disheveled blonde mess of hair that is Nat.

She's rubbing the sleep out of her eyes, a yawn spilling from her lips before anything else. "Vika? Sorry, saw you called, was mid-puking my internal organs out, what's up?"

"What's up? What's up with the fucking fish more like it. How did she even get a fish in my apartment? Did she Mission Impossible her way inside? What am I supposed to do with a fish, Nat?"

Her green eyes widen at the word-vomit that's been rapidly building inside of me on the trip over. Her mouth opens to answer, but then either thinks better or finds nothing to say, and instead she steps to the side and gestures towards the living room. I all but barge through the doorway inside.

Mark's completely enveloped in Nat's pastel pink comforter, cuddled up on one side of the couch and peeking out at my entrance. Judging by the dark circles under his eyes and the uncharacteristic grimace on his face, he's probably suffering a similar fate to Nat. Still, my empathy is short-lived as I dump myself next to him, arms crossed over my chest.

"Your sister is actively destroying my life, Mark. Genuinely taking a massive crap all over it. I'm taking hours after a lunch break at Chipotle proportions."

He sniffs. "Just agree. Your life will be so much easier if you just agree."

I throw a pointed look to Nat, who's collapsing into one of the offset recliners. "This is why you agreed to marry him, isn't it?"

"Well, that and obviously his massive di-"

"Alright, I'm here to talk about the fish, and also I slept with Noel, but that's second to the intruder in my house. Or, Mark's house. My life," I amend with a huff, breath short, an anxious buzzing under my skin.

Nat's unfazed by my dramatics, but arches a brow at Noel's name. "Why are you here, then? Shouldn't you be drowning in post-sex bliss right now? I mean, you're the one that wanted this."

My stomach churns at the thought. Instead, I heave a tired sigh, shoulders tense, unresolved frustration prickling at the back of my neck.

"Cecilia has a key to my house," Mark croaks out for explanation, "There's probably fish food in one of the cupboards. Like I said, just agree."

"None of those are appropriate reactions to what I'm saying here, oh my god. There's a fish that I must now take care of because you," I say, pointing to Nat, "insist on trying to make Mark's mom like you and you," now I'm pointing to Mark, "had to go and have a sister. Both of you, terrible job. Zero out of ten."

I'm swallowing a bitter dryness that's unfurled on my tongue. Dark eyes are flashing in the back of my mind.

There's a split-second where I wonder if he'll follow me where, through the process of elimination and my lack of funds I'm sure he could guess I am, but then realize that the thought is probably mine alone. I'm not even sure if I'd want him to, either. Not that I'm an excellent judge of character for what I want, apparently.

"I'm pretty hungover, but I don't think you're making any sense. Please translate this Vika speak into normal people talk." Nat's rubbing her forehead, nose crinkled, tired notes weighing down her voice.

"I don't have a house or a legitimate career or even any prospects for the future. How am I supposed to take care of a fish, Nat?"

There's a beat of quiet, where Mark has once again poked his head out of his blanket cocoon with half-coherent concern, and Nat's green gaze is searching my face. Then she's nodding her head with a hum.

"Alright, this I can translate. You're freaking out about what the fish means, I get it. Mark go pour us some coffee, I already made a pot." She waves off the man, gaze never straying from mine.

He makes a noise of protest. "What? Why? I like it here, I'm barely over the spins."

"Coffee, babe. Two milk, one sugar. Please and thank you." Nat's sharp gaze snaps to him.

Whatever room left for argument in her voice is immediately murdered by her eyes, and Mark's surrendering himself to a standing position, still draping the blanket over his shoulders with a stubborn determination that trails after him on his way out. I'm watching with mild curiosity until Nat snaps her fingers in my face and steals my attention.

"You're spiralling," she says, brows raised. "What's up? Why're you all heated all of a sudden? If it's about a place, I can help you find somewh-"

"That's it!" I cry out, hands shaking. "I'm twenty-four years old and I still need everyone to hold my hand through being a proper adult! I mean, I can't keep playing the orphan card-"

"It's a pretty reasonable card to have, Vi," she interjects.

I sigh, murky thoughts of my parents from years ago circling my head like morbid blue birds, shoulders dropping just as fast as my will to keep going. But I defiantly shake my head of them. "You helped me get the job, Mark's letting me stay at his place, these pants- Nat, these are Cavalli."

Her eyes widen to saucers, voice dropping. "Vika, did you steal those?"

"No!" I snap, scalp prickling at the accusation, more because it almost feels as if I have. "They're Noel's sister's, he let me borrow them. But that's what I mean, what am I even doing here? Hanging out with Noel in Mark's apartment, staring at fish, what's even happening? How is Mark of all people funding this surreal life of mine?"

As if on cue, Mark steps through the doorway, the blanket still superman-style on his shoulders and two mugs of piping hot coffee in his hands, steam coiling about the rims. He pads over to gently place the cups on the coffee table and throws me a small smile.

"Alexei's grandma owns the place, that's why we got such a good deal on it. You seriously don't have to worry about rent or anything. I mean, I'd keep it, but Nat and I agreed to live closer to both our work. You're not putting me out at all, but, uh, Alexei has someone new moving in the first of next month."

Mark's face is tight as if it pains him to kick me out of his own apartment that he still funds despite stepping through only a couple times a week, and it probably does, which pinches at my heart even more. He falls back next to me on the couch and I draw a deep breath.

"No, no, stop being so nice. I'm going to find my own place- alone. Without your help, or Nat's help, or N-"

My tongue's in place to finish the name, but the air is cut short in my throat, stopped by something I'm not quite sure, and I let it die instead. Nat's eyes are drinking me in, scrutinizing in a way that's familiar after all these years, probably better versed in my micro expressions than even I am. I try to smooth my face out. There's knowing to know.

"Did you up and run out? Did you even say anything to Noel or did you book it?" Nat asks, reaching to grab one of the steamy mugs and cradling it with both her hands. The accusation is softened by her eyes. "Does Noel even know you're here?"

I push my tongue against the inside of my cheek. "Well, uh, yes?"

Mark shifts next to me, perking up at the mention of his best friend. "Did you just leave him confused?"

"Well, confused probably. Generally unimpressed with my existence, more likely," I admit, wrinkling my nose. "I left on... weird terms. I don't know."

"Is he okay?" Mark asks, piqued interest settling him into a more upright position.

"Well, I mean, I guess so," I say, shrugging. "Probably."

"No- did he look okay, Vika? Are you sure? Did you see?"

As Mark's interrogating gaze drills into me, I parch, sputtering out some more semi-coherent reassurances, drowning in maybe and probably and hesitance. There's an intensity that I'm unfamiliar with on his face.

Nat clicks her tongue, catching my attention in a way that's a small breath of relief. She's fixing Mark with a pointed stare. "Hey, it's fine. No reason to use the third degree. He's an adult, a really weird one, but still over the age of twenty-five. He'll be okay." She shoots me a small smile of camaraderie.

My head tilts back. "Weren't you the one that wasn't on board with me talking to him in the first place?"

"Don't think this is getting you out of grandpa duty, Vika," she says, grinning. "You'll be hearing stories about mother Russia until you're literally begging for ol' Vlad to poison you out of your misery."

I turn my head when a troubled sigh falls from Mark's mouth, who's rubbing small circles into his temples. "You guys don't get Noel, okay?"

"There's nothing to be troubled over," I reassure him, flashing him a brief smile. "Seriously, he was busy with work. Anyway, if you mentioned it, I don't even think he'd remember."

At this point, I'm unsure of who I'm really trying to convince.

Mark doesn't seem entirely persuaded, but that could be the left-over tequila that's still making its way through his system, and only relents with a soft grunt. I can't help the prickle of curiosity in the back of my throat.

"Why do you think he'll care so much?"

The words feel awkward in my mouth, and when I catch Nat's eye we both know there's more to my question than what's on the surface, but I don't add any follow up.

"It's Noel," Mark says as if it's answer enough itself, which to someone who is continually bewildered by every single interaction with the man is not, but Mark adds nothing else. Instead, he pushes the covers off of him and lifts to his feet, stretching, and says, "I'm gonna go call him."

"Or," Nat cuts in, dragging it out with a small smile. "You could also go over there, since I don't think Vika wants to go back to your place tonight." She's still holding the mug with both her hands and takes a small sip. "Only a suggestion."

Mark freezes, frowning. "But we were supposed to watch Love Actually tonight."

I snort, and Nat reaches over to give me a chastising smack on the arm.

"Babe, we'll watch it tomorrow, I promise," she assures him, and he's still wearing that injured look, but nods.

As he treks out of the room, I have to distract myself with my own mug of coffee to stop from bursting out laughing.

"I'm really going to find a place, I promise. All on my own," I tell Nat once I've sobered up a bit, and take a small, relieving sip of caffeine. "Without any of your guys' help."

She raises her brows at me, sending me a look over her mug. "And this is only about the place? That's it? Nothing else on your mind?"

I shake my head, gaze snapping to the floor. "What are you talking about?" I tsk, waving her off. "This is completely about the place, and that's it."

She hums as if she isn't entirely convinced, but she drops the subject and picks up the remote that's next to her instead. I'm shifting in my seat when she flicks on an episode of Friends, and I ignore the way that her question lingers, breathing on the back of my neck.

It's as Mark's waving us goodbye in the doorway, reminding us that there's leftover pizza in the fridge when I feel an unusual vibration against my thigh. My gaze immediately snaps to Nat, but she's distracted by blowing her fiancé a kiss. My heart does a double-tap when I lift my phone to see a familiar name written across it.

Fed the fish and left the apartment. You can come back.

A precarious swirl of emotion rises in my chest, and I stare at Noel's message, reading it three times in a row before it even begins to make any sense to me. Nat mentions something about going to get some pizza from the kitchen, but it sounds too far away to matter. I frown.

I'm really sorry for freaking out, I don't kn|

Pause. Erase.

The fish thing was weird, sorry about tha|

Pause Erase.

Thanks man. Appreciate it.

I consider sending a smiley face for good measure, but figure that it probably doesn't matter to Noel anyway, and click send.

chapter twenty one

"I CAN'T TELL if moving in with three guys is gonna be more like a fun sitcom situation, or if I'm actually going to get murdered," I say into the phone pressed against my ear, using the other hand with my half-full coffee cup to push open the front doors of Mark's complex. "The rent isn't half bad though, for the city at least."

There's a dull ache in my legs from bouncing around town all day, various addresses still jumbled up in my mind, but it's mediated by a kindling sense of accomplishment. It's more than just overpriced caffeine that brings a little more spirit in my step, and I even flash Mark's pretentious in-finance neighbour a brief smile when I pass him to the elevator. Which he doesn't return, but whatever.

I'm going to be not homeless. He can suck my semi-financially stable dick.

"Did they seem nice?" Nat asks on the other end of the line.

Stepping through the elevator doors, I hum. "Well, yeah, but so did Ted Bundy, and he murdered over 30 women."

"I don't think you have to worry about being serial murdered, Vika. I would worry about more how often they clean their bathrooms."

I roll my eyes and press Mark's floor number, 32, reminded that it might be one of the last times. "Listen, college girls are one of prime target groups for serial murder, so maybe we should be talking about what's actually important here. Like my life."

Nat snorts. "You're 24 and you dropped out."

I sniff, offended. "First of all, rude. Second of all, I get carded all the time. The Chinese side is gonna keep this face smooth until I hit 70, and then I will go full walnut. Until then, fuck you." As I'm stepping out into the hallway, my fingertips instinctively reach to the corner of my eye where I'm sure my lack of a healthy sleep schedule is doing no favours, but I pray genetics will pull me through.

I'm not sure if rooming with three men would help or hurt my potential crow's feet situation, but I figure my beer pong game will be upped at least three levels, and that's always a handy skill to keep tucked away. If I'm not brutally maimed and shoved in a trunk, that is.

Nat laughs as I pat my pockets down in search of keys. "If they call you back, you should probably go for it. Better them than the girl who has five cats."

"I don't know what you mean, I'm pretty sure Cleo is actually starting to lik- holy shit."

I pause mid-swing of the door, still clutching the handle as Noel and I lock eyes. He's wearing a look that's bushy-tailed and staring down a speeding car, cat bundled up in his arms. I'm frozen and a strange noise I can't remember ever making sounds in the back of my throat.

"Oh my god, did the cat attack you? Vika, I told you not to antagonise it! Are you okay?" Nat's panicky and concerned voice is sharp in the receiver, but it's easily drowned out by my heart beating a tattoo in my chest.

"It's not the cat," I reassure her, watching as Noel drops Cleo to the floor, feet still planted where I'd found him. "Physically, I am fine. I'll give you a mental update later, but I would prepare with at least two bottles of pinot. Talk to you later."

When I click the phone off, cutting Nat mid-threat to tell her what's going on, Noel's carding a hand through his hair.

"I-"

"I-"

We both start at once and then stop together the same. There's a moment of hesitation where we're waiting for the other to continue, and I nod for him to go on first.

Noel clears his throat, and I ignore the way his Adam's apple dips in his throat. Judging by the way he stuffs his hands in his pockets, I doubt he knows what to do with them. I'm still gripping a little too hard to my coffee too, spurred by the weird intensity burning behind his thick frames, and I swallow.

"Mark said you'd be out, that's why I- sorry, I didn't think you'd be here," he explains, shifting in his spot. "You're supposed to be house hunting."

I pointedly ignore the way he looks in the soft blue button-down, which is fantastic, obviously, and instead focus on Cleo darting into one of the other rooms. "Yeah, I've found some pretty promising places," I say, scratching the back of my head as I meet his eyes once again. "At this point it's either prime-time television, getting cannibalised, or bust."

Noel nods, his mouth twitching as if he's unsure of what to do with this information, which- understandable. "Right, well, I'll be taking my leave. Sorry again." The guard that's protecting his unreadable expression reverberates in his clipped tone.

"Wait," I stop him, against all my shrieking instincts, throwing up a hand as he moves to brush by me. His brows climb up in confusion, and I ignore the small part of me that's in resounding agreement. "Listen, I'm not sure if you forgot but there's a wedding coming up fast and Nat will actually murder me if I make it weird with-" I hesitate, gesturing vaguely between us as all possible words seem to completely dissipate, "this."

He nods, apparently understanding what this means despite the ghost of a frown on his face. "Talking might be good." His words and his face don't seem to be on the same page.

As I take the lead towards the living room, he trails obediently after me without a word, and it's quiet as I set my coffee and oversized purse on the small table. The nerves in the atmosphere are amplified by distant memories of both of us between these four walls, on that navy blue sectional. It's almost strange how our entire relationship has unfurled between these decorative throw pillows. I pointedly shove the thought Challenger Deep when we sit a respectable distance, facing each other.

When I open my mouth, Noel beats me to it. "I'm sorry," he says, and I'm surprised by the uncharacteristically tender notes in his voice. "About the fish. I understand now that I was being... condescending."

I wrinkle my nose, shoulders climbing up in agreement. "Well, I can't say you're wrong," I murmur, but when I see the genuine flicker in his dark eyes, I falter. "I might have also been a little over dramatic too."

It's then that his phone vibrates, and I can't tell if it's saving me from the conversation or not yet, but I let out a small breath as he reaches to grab it. However, it's short-lived as Noel barely glances at the screen and shuts it down, slipping it back into his pocket. I open my mouth to ask if that's a good idea, but then close it again.

He still says nothing, though, gaze lingering on my face in a way that magnifies the quiet, and I can't stop my mouth from moving to fill the space. "It's been, um, well, a lot," I continue. "Everything kinda felt like it was all happening at once, and I got overwhelmed. I know, me? Victoria Phan? Doesn't have everything together? We were all so fooled."

"What overwhelmed you?" he asks, a frown still tugging down the corner of his mouth.

I pause, the weight of all the things I can't quite put into words pressing on my chest. "Just a lot of things," I supplement instead. "It's not a problem, seriously, don't worry about it."

"I can help, if you'd let me."

Quiet floods between us as I drink in his creased brow, the distance between us having dwindled sometimes during conversation. His frown seems to be triggered more of concern than his usual inherent disapproval of all things, and I can only manage a few seconds of eye contact before my pulse trips over itself to get away.

"No, no, seriously Noel," I say, shaking my head, aggressively looking everywhere but his face. "You don't have to, especially only because I'm Mark's friend- seriously. I got this. Remember the probably not homeless thing from before? That's a thing that's, uh, not a thing anymore. So we're peachy keen."

My mouth feels dry, and when I reach for the coffee, I'm disappointed that the rest is lukewarm and not at all comforting to my situation. Spending five dollars on a coffee now seems extravagant when I have to start saving in case of an early funeral, that is from serial murder or potentially my inability to wade through the anxiety of this situation.

Whichever one got me first.

"I want to help," he insists, and there's something arresting about his gaze that causes me to still. "For me."

I clear my throat, eyes widening. "Seriously, stop trying to force your ten thousand dollars on me, I'm not going to accept it," I joke, forcing an unsure smile on my face. "I've already Julia Roberts'd myself."

The edge of his mouth quirks up in a way that allows me to breathe again, and it's the first break to the tense air we're both drowning in.

"I mean it," he says, the intensity a little less overpowering. "You just have to ask."

I don't have the resolve to piece together what that means in the grand scheme of things, where we fell on the spectrum of relationships or if we even appeared on one at all, what was reflected in those dark browns eyes- the question, ironically enough, dies on my tongue. I think back to Nat's wedding, the promises I'd made, the disappointment I knew that would follow once the chapter closed, and we all resumed our regularly scheduled lives.

Apart.

And asking meant actualising the hope I'd been so stubbornly swallowing down, and my quota of adulthood had already been filled for the month.

"All I am asking for you is to not act like a fucking weirdo around me, yeah? I mean, not anymore than you usually are. Just the regularly accepted amount of bizarreness."

Noel looks positively affronted. "I am not weird," he insists, lips parted in disbelief and drawing a laugh from mine.

"Of course, of course," I mockingly placate him, patting his shoulder, and then, dropping my voice a few octaves and straightening my spine, "I must take my leave now."

He's fighting back a smile. "That's a terrible impression of me."

I gasp. "Cleo thinks it's a great impression."

"Cleopatra," he corrects, almost automatically, and when I meet his gaze, something softens in my shoulders.

The quiet that overtakes us is a bit more comfortable, and I take the moment to let my eyes linger, fall from the highs of his cheekbones to the dip of his Cupid's bow and I can't tell if it's my mind playing tricks on me, but we're growing closer. My initial plan of un-complicating everything is falling behind thoughts of how warm his mouth is, and the heat of his palms spreading against the small of my back, and how easily I unravel under his touch.

Before I can convolute the situation, though, there's a resounding knock on the door that makes both of us jump. I blink, shaking my head in a way that I hope shakes away those traitorous thoughts, but Noel's already up on his feet.

"Who is it?" I ask after his figure, brows knitted.

"I have no id-" he begins, but then is promptly cut off as he swings the door open and is shoved unceremoniously out of the way.

"I've been calling your phone all morning," the dark-haired girl complains, shaking her hands in irritation. "How have you not picked up? You're practically married to that thing."

I wonder if there's something genetic about the Carltons that predisposes them to barging into other people's homes, considering the pattern.

She looks casual in that painfully gorgeous off-duty model way, with a bright white t-shirt and boyfriend jeans, dark hair cascading over her shoulders in effortless waves. Whatever genetics caused an indifference to others' privacy also seemed to carry cheekbones that could cut glass, apparently.

"Angelica, what are you doing here?" Noel's voice comes out more of a demand than a question.

She rolls her eyes. "Well, I couldn't get a hold of you and you're always hiding yourself in this apartment, so I thought I'd try my chances. Maybe if you answered your phone I wouldn't have to parade around town looking for- oh."

She stops, mid-thought, when her eyes fall on me, still frozen on the couch. Confusion marks her tanned face. I say nothing and throw a silent hand up in acknowledgement.

"Who's this?" she asks, tilting her head. "Are you here to clean?"

At least I didn't get mistaken for a sex worker twice.

"I'm-" I begin, but Noel's quicker and he's already swept across the room to come as a physical barrier between us, arms up and already ushering Angelica through the door.

She isn't easily ushered, though, and her eyebrows knit as she tries to gain a better look at me around his reach. "Why are you being so weird?" she asks, sending him a pointed glance. "I was only asking."

"She's nobody, Angelica. Now go, I'll call you a cab, and you can tell me whatever you need in the car."

Nobody. Nobody. The rest of his sentiment is drowned out by the word, echoing continuously in my mind, torturously growing louder in my ears. Nobody. Something inexplicable sinks deep inside of me, frozen wildfire spreading through my veins. I swallow, hard. Nobody.

It's a confirmation of what I already knew this entire time, but somehow it's more painful coming from his lips. All those whispers from Christina's party, left underneath those maple trees in the park, the outside world I'd always tried to deny.

"Noel!" Angelica chastises, slapping him lightly on the arm with the back of her hand. "She's a professional, don't be rude!"

He turns when he sees that her eyes have caught attention, but I'm already on my feet, my movements running on instinct alone. I brush by them quickly, ignoring the tightness in my throat and the heat behind my eyes, pausing only briefly in the door.

"This nobody will be taking her leave now, don't worry," I reassure him with a small, insincere smile, the words like frost on my tongue and barely reaching a note of the cold in my eyes. We catch a fleeting glance, but I don't linger, not anymore, and turn to leave.

"Vika- I didn't- wait!" His voice carries down the hall, but my pace refuses to slow, fingernails biting into the palms of my hands, and I'm gone.

chapter twenty two

"I DON'T KNOW WHO you think you're trying to fool here, but that is not Perrier," the dark-haired woman says in a clipped tone, thin lips pressed together, unimpressed. Her eyes narrow.

I blink. "I'm sorry, what? That- that is Perrier."

She rolls her eyes as if responding is a waste of precious breath, and I have to take a quick survey of the restaurant to make that sure she's talking to me, and not an actual toddler. Not that the annoyance on her face can make the distinction. When I continue to stand there, silent and absolutely bewildered, she heaves a sigh.

"Are you trying to imply I don't know what Perrier tastes like?" She arches a pointed brow.

"Of course not," I blurt out, eyes widening. "I just- with all due respect, I poured the drink straight from the bottle at your table. And the bottle is still right next to your glass. That is, um, that's Perrier."

When I gesture to the bottle of Perrier that is, for everyone to see, sitting dutifully next to her glass, she clicks her tongue. I wonder if it's her hair drawn so tightly into the bun piled on her head, or maybe an after-effect of the Botox that has given her temporary blindness. Any other reasonable explanation escapes me.

"I don't know what kind of operation you're running here, but I know what Perrier tastes like, and this is not Perrier," she says, low and sharp, venom in her eyes as they lock onto mine. "Now, I don't want to speak to your manager, but-"

"I will definitely grab you another unopened bottle and bring it here," I quickly reassure her, hands formed into fists by my sides. The thought of Christian's steely eyes draws shivers down my spine, still recovering from the accidentally-shattering-an-entire-bottle-of-Cristal incident, name self-explanatory. "And I'd like to sincerely apologize for this upset."

She leans back, apparently satisfied with this answer, and flashes me a predatory look. "And it's ruined my meal."

The polite smile is frozen on my face and only enduring through sheer will-power alone. "Of course, of course, I'll see what I can do about getting some of it compensated, and free dessert as well. For the pain we've caused. My apologies, again," I manage through gritted teeth.

Suddenly I was all types of on board with whatever Karl Marx had to say. The bourgeoisie can suck a dick.

"At the minimum," she adds, brows climbing up her chemically-smoothed forehead in a challenge.

I have to turn on my heel and stalk away to stop myself from going absolutely mental on this sixty-five-year-old woman that I'm absolutely positive I could best in a physical confrontation if necessary. Despite finally warming up to the POS system, the table numbers, and the natural flow of work at Viva La Breakfast, the clientele still makes me want to legitimately orchestrate a revolution.

And that includes both current and past patrons, honestly. Not that thinking about particular dark-haired and brown-eyed men is helping calm me down at all.

There's a groan climbing up my throat when I return to the server station, pressing the woman's table with a little more force than necessary on the screen. I barely even notice when Malia, the other server working, slides in behind me until she's peeking over my shoulder.

"I totally knew that she was gonna pull something from the second she walked in," she says, sighing. "You should've heard her last week-she was throwing a fit because she couldn't bring in her little rat of a dog."

I snort, turning to face the dark-haired girl. "Thank god she thinks our operation is only pouring non-Perrier water into Perrier bottles and not a total front for money laundering. She is really keeping our city safe."

"There is no way she can be that much a total bitch and not get off on it sexually. There has to be a sexual component." Malia laughs, all dimples and red lips.

I grin, and it's one of the first in a couple of days but almost always promised on a shift with her. If anything, Malia's almost constant commentary on the upscale patrons of Viva is the only thing getting me through this shift, not that I'm particularly looking forward to it to ending, either. There's a text lingering on my phone from Mark, updating me that I can just drop off the key on the kitchen counter when I finally pack up my things.

I'd barely swept through the apartment since I'd made my, yet again, dramatic exit, and I genuinely did not feel like making my not-so-triumphant return.

As I'm punching in the discount for the lady's smoked salmon and steamed eggs, Malia's leaning against the counter and eyeing the restaurant. I shoot her a confused glance when she hums.

"Speaking of sexy," she murmurs, smirking. "You've got a new arrival in your section."

I roll my eyes, tightening the apron that's slung around my waist. "I don't care what they look like as long as they don't accuse me of forgery."

Malia laughs, and it distracts me until I step around the corner, and then my heart instantly plummets.

It's with a sharp gasp and wide eyes that I scramble back into the corner of the station, cursing under my breath. Malia fixes me with a weird look, frowning. "You okay?"

"Can you take that table?" I all but beg, hands clasped together as I add a, "Please?"

She arches a brow, skeptical. "Bad tipper? Or bad ex-boyfriend?"

I pause for a moment, because none of those truly encompass the weird dance that Noel and I have, or had, I guess. The non-relationship of our relationship doesn't really seem to fit in the cute little boxes she offers- I could only wish.

"Uhh, the second," I haphazard, not even bothering to try to explain the semantics. "I'd seriously owe you so much. He's a fantastic tipper- no stress, it'll be great."

She taps her chin thoughtfully.

"I'll pay you five dollars- ten dollars!" I insist, my voice growing vaguely more hysterical. "I'll cover any of your shifts!"

When we lock eyes, she loses her composure and dissolves into laughter, waving me off. "Oh, stop being a fool. You just gotta say ex and I got you." She flashes me a grin.

When her mop of curly, dark hair vanishes from my sight, I can finally take a much-needed breath. My pulse is still thudding in my ears, a reminder that only a few feet away is Noel, who I haven't seen since the day before, when he'd had the audacity to call me a nobody. There's been complete radio silence on both ends- to both my disdain and pleasure.

I swallow my nerves and swipe up a bottle of Perrier.

Despite my pointed attempts not to peer in Noel's direction, his dark eyes scorching into me as I make an obvious detour around his booth to get to table six, the fateful home of Perrier-not-Perrier lady. And his burning gaze refuses to let up as I make a painfully stilted demonstration of me opening the Perrier bottle and pouring her another glass, which she takes a sip from with contempt written all over her face.

It passes, at least, and she waves me away to get her the free dessert. All with Noel burning holes into the back of my head.

The blatantly ignoring tactic doesn't prove all that successful, as Malia mentions that Noel specifically asks for me, and despite my almost palpable avoidance, he stays. Half an hour later and he's still stubbornly tucked away into the booth, two coffee refills down and nearing a third judging by the way he's been taking sips every few moments. Or at least, from what I can see in my peripherals.

As I jab my finger into the system screen, ordering a coffee with a little too much force, Malia's leaning against the counter. Her arms are folded over her chest, and when I peek over there's a frown tugging down the corners of her mouth.

"Do you want me to call the police or something? Is he stalking you, Vika?" she asks, concern creasing her brow.

I heave a sigh. "No, no, he isn't- I'll talk to him. Don't worry about it, I got it covered."

She hums as if she isn't entirely convinced, and internally, I agree. Still, I square my shoulders and settle my nerves, turning towards Noel's table to find him unsurprisingly gazing back behind those thick frames. For a moment I'm called back to all those times I was basically shrieking for his attention, for him to look back at me, just to catch a glimpse of myself in those dark pupils, but now I'm wishing for anything but.

Despite his lingering presence, he looks genuinely shocked when I slide into the seat opposite of him. I pointedly smooth out my face to not give him any wrong impressions, such as I want to be here, that I want to talk to him, and that I am okay with what he said. Because I am not, and there's a trickle of irritation at the base of my spine when it plays back in my mind.

Nobody.

"You're freaking out Malia. She thinks you're a stalker and she wants to call the cops on you," I say, fixing him with a deadpan.

His eyes widen. "I don't- what? I'm not- I'm not a stalker. I just wanted to talk to you. Vika, I just-"

"Most people would probably send a text," I cut him off, voice cold. "Not sure if you knew that thing," I gesture to his phone, "It can actually send messages to other people's phone. Most people do that instead of, you know, stalking someone's place of work."

"I'm not-" he protests, but then when he meets my gaze, quickly seems to realise it's a losing battle. The bags under his eyes are a little darker than usual, now that I can see him up close. His hair a touch more dishevelled, unsurprising, as he cards his hands through it again. "I didn't know what to say."

I blink. "So instead you came here to say nothing? Solid plan. Great job. You can leave now."

There's something strikingly defenseless in his dark brown eyes, uncharacteristic to all I've ever seen of him, and I can almost feel something waver inside of me, drawn by the vulnerability. The frustrated sigh he gives, more to himself than anything, has me wanting to reach over and soothe it, but I don't.

I steel my resolve instead.

"I wanted to apologize to you directly. You have to understand I didn't mean it the way it came out. You're not a nobody. I didn't- I wasn't thinking when I said it," he explains, voice soft, trailing off at the end as he studies my face. "I'm sorry, Vika."

There's a beat of quiet, where his apology is still in the air, sinks in, crumbles into dust.

"I don't have to understand anything," I say, looking away. "You said what you said, and whatever you meant, it doesn't matter. Who were we kidding, anyway? It's better we just left it where it ended off. Let's not pretend it was going to last after the wedding."

His brows pull in as he pauses. "It wasn't." The end of his sentence lilts up, as if in question, and searches for some sort of reply but doesn't find anything. He doesn't follow it up, and I don't either. The answer had always been written out, clear as crystal, branded all over everything we ever were. Temporary, momentary, fleeting.

"It wasn't," I echo, ignoring the way it presses against my chest. "Bye, Noel."

I slip out of the booth, ignoring the prickle at my eyes and the catch in my throat. There's a burning that's crawling up from my stomach, but I shove it back down. Just as I grit my teeth, though, there's a grip on my wrist that's pulling me back.

"Vika, wait-"

"What the fuck do you want, Noel?" I snap, cheeks warm, hands shaking as I rip my wrist from his grasp. I pin him with a glare. He shrinks away from it, as if it's physically burning him. "And don't say you don't know, because I don't either, so maybe you should just leave."

This seems to be the one thing that resonates, because he nods. With his head down and a murmur of something I don't quite catch, he's grabbing his jacket and leaving a couple of bills on the table, and then he's gone.

There's a moment where I'm not sure how to feel, the mess of emotions too conflicted to even begin sorting through, but when I turn to see Christian with his arms crossed over his chest, a fresh wave of anxiety crashes into me. A quick survey of the restaurant has me realising that my little outburst hadn't been as intimate as I'd thought, with a few customers still shooting curious glances in my direction. I draw a deep breath and trudge back towards the server's station.

"My office," Christian demands, voice rough, before he's off.

Malia shoots me a sympathetic look, nose wrinkled. "Babe, I'm so sorry," she murmurs. "One of the cooks is going for a Starbucks run, I'll grab you something."

I mumble a quick thanks before begrudgingly following after Christian into his office, shoving down all my hysterical instincts, realizing that I'm screwing up one of the few things actually going right in my life- and now I'm going to be fired.

Christian's already settled in his chair, hands folded in front of him on the desk that separates us. I settle into the seat opposite of him, and while I'm usually comforted by his light blue eyes or the salt and pepper of his hair, there's a tickle of nausea in the back of my throat. Which probably wouldn't help my not getting fired case all that much.

Maybe I could blame the flu.

"I'm so sorry," I burst out before he can say anything, voice coming out more like a squeak than anything. "I'm truly, genuinely, I'm so sorry, Christian. I didn't mean to make a scene."

He heaves a sigh, emphasizing the lines on his face. "Vika, it's important to always be professional, even if this is only a restaurant. It's about image."

"I agree!" I add too quickly. "I just had- it was a lapse in judgement. I'm really sorry."

He pauses for a moment, scanning my face, and then his shoulders drop. "I don't want to let you go- you've picked up on everything at this point, with only a few, minor incidents, and you're not a bad worker. But you can't do this sort of thing, especially with customers. You can't let your personal issues reflect badly on the restaurant."

I swallow hard, and flex my jaw, an uncomfortable heat crawling all over my body. "I promise, I won't, Christian. I won't let you down. I'll do anything- I love this job, I want to work here, please."

There's a frown still etched on his face. "You're done for today- cool your head. Come back in next shift with this resolved. And Vika, we don't deal with third chances here."

"Thank you! Thank you so much, Christian! Nothing like this will ever happen again!" I promise, nodding my head frantically as I pick myself up and restraining my urge to tackle him into a hug. "I'll make sure of it."

He shoots me a small smile and then gestures towards the door, which I take as my exit and escape. There's a dangerous mix of emotions bubbling up inside of me, threatening to rupture into the chaos that's mirrored outside, but I swallow it down as I finish up with my tables. Then, with a quick goodbye to Malia who's passing along my coffee with a warm hug, I'm stumbling out the doors of Viva la Breakfast onto the bustling street.

And if I wipe a few stray tears away with my sleeve on the bus ride home, well, no one's there to see it. No one that matters, anyway.

chapter twenty three

IT'S DARK WHEN I push open the door to Mark's apartment. The idle notes of twilight are painted across the floor-to-ceiling windows, purples and indigos spilling into one another, offering little light. The rest of the room is in shadows, all shapes and figures that are all-too familiar after months of living here. My hand lifts to flick on the light switch, hovers for a moment, but then stops.

I don't mind the dark right now.

My feet lead me to the guest bedroom where I quickly drop my purse off next to my stuffed-to-the-brim and poorly organised luggage, then find myself drawn back to the living room.

As I collapse onto the couch, a sense of uncanny overwhelms me. The standard fixtures are all in place- the couch, the counters, the lamps and whatnot, but different. The human touches have all been stolen. The TV is gone, the framed photo of Mark and Nat, the soft blanket I had thrown over the couch. It's strikingly empty.

My mind wanders to the almost clinical atmosphere that had also greeted me at Noel's apartment, but I don't linger so long to figure out what that means.

There's still an almost constant stinging in the back of my eyes, which only seems to grow now that I'm no longer in anyone's line of sight. I try to grit my teeth, look up to the ceiling, mash my lips together to keep myself dry, but there's still one betraying tear that spills over. It rolls down my cheek, and with a sniff, I wipe it away with my sleeve.

There are clearly more important things I have to be upset about-my looming student debt, barely escaping homelessness, the situation in Aleppo. The options are endless. Noel should've been the last thing on my mind.

Nobody.

It isn't fair that the word had left his mouth, a manifestation of all my fears smashed and pulverized into that six letter word. That a five-minute confrontation could reduce me to tears when I hadn't cried over anybody, let alone a man in years.

The most I felt after ending it with Chad was a little annoyed because I'd left my favourite bra there.

And Vika Phan doesn't cry, I tell myself, fighting back another onslaught of prickles behind my eyelashes. Especially not sober, which I'm reminded that I painfully am, and lean back into the couch cushions.

My attention is caught by my phone next to me, Nat's name lighting up the darkness. A part of me knows that if I answer she'll be over in less than twenty minutes, holding a tub of ice cream and a bag of flamin' hot Cheetos, arms open and ready for me to collapse into, but I still don't answer. I heave a tired sigh, instead, watching as it goes dark again.

If it's five minutes or forty-five, I'm not sure, but I sit there staring into nothing, somehow both disturbed and comforted by the absolute lack of anything in sight. My mind wanders from high school to Noel's bed to the still unfinished manuscript that's been lingering on my laptop for years too long. Trying to figure out when the inherent compass of life that everyone else seems to be built with ended up broken inside of me. Why everyone's north star seemed to be like a magnet pulling them forward and I was a much less successful groundhog day horror.

It's movement that drags me from my reverie, a flash of colour that punches my heart into my throat. With my breath already stolen, I realise it's Cleo slowly meandering her way towards me, green eyes shimmering in the dark.

I watch, mildly curious, expecting her to walk her way towards and then around me like she usually does, maintaining that ever-cautious five foot distance.

But she doesn't.

I make a half-human noise as she hops up next to me on the couch, looking as guarded as a cat can be. I blink to make sure that my eyes aren't playing tricks on me, even more when she waltzes straight onto my lap, all beauty and grace, curling up as if I was more of a satin pillow than a human being.

There's a beat of complete and total silence. I'm frozen, eyes-wide, waiting for Cleo to seize the opportunity and tear my face off from close range, but she doesn't. She sits, comfortable, quiet. After my lungs begin to burn, I take a breath.

When I get used to the new weight on my lap, I relax. I don't pet her, trying to keep my eyes inside of my skull where they belong, thank you very much, but I enjoy the warmth of her body against my thighs. My disastrous lack of sideburns tells me I shouldn't read too much into it, but I can't pull back the fresh wave of tears that come with the heat of another living creature next to me.

"Thank you, Cleopatra," I murmur, sniffing. "I know that technically he's your owner and if he walked in right now, you'd bound into his arms but I kind of feel you're taking my side right now and that's basically one of the best things that has happened to me in for the past week."

Cleo, like usual, doesn't say anything. Nevertheless, it's still comforting. So much so that when she finally stretches and sits up, hopping back onto the ground and stealing the warmth away with her, it takes all my willpower not to grab and drag her back into my arms.

"You can run away but you can't run away from the fact that we had a moment, Cleo!" I call after her retreating figure, not that she cares. "You can't run from the truth!"

I try not to be offended that the fish is better company than I am, and then I remember- the fish. The guest bedroom door left slightly ajar from earlier springs up to memory.

"Don't touch the fish!" I all but shriek as I immediately jump to my feet and charge after her, eyes wide. "I swear if you buttered me up to eat my friend, Cleo!"

I slam my palm against the door frame to steady myself, chest heaving, breath short. Cleo's eyes snap to mine, absent from both innocence or guilt. She's delicately poised on my desk, ears perked up and facing the fish bowl that I've left on the dresser- the highest point in the room.

I narrow my eyes. "Cleo, you cannot eat the fish."

All sanity aside, I swear she narrows her eyes in a challenge.

"Shoo, shoo," I say while waving her off my desk, and she obliges, but not without glaring green-eyed daggers in my direction. "This changes nothing!"

When her black and tan striped tail disappears around the corner, I'm left standing in the room I've called home for the past couple of months. All my belongings have been shoved and zipped away, my entire life in two suitcases and a backpack, excluding my laptop, which sits on my desk where Cleo had been.

I try not to think about the Cavalli jeans that are stowed away somewhere, too soft for me to throw away on principle.

Crinkling my nose, I sit down on the desk chair I'd been avoiding for weeks, fingers brushing over the cool aluminium of my laptop. Nobody seems to be synonymous with another seven lettered bane of my existence- failure. And as I lift the laptop open and boot it up, welcomed to a word document that had been first created years ago, all thirteen of them weigh heavier in the pit of my stomach.

"All right, Fish, you watch me," I say to the splash of indigo swimming around on my dresser, stretching my back and cracking my knuckles in determination. "You might need money to do a lot of things in this world, but writing is free, and I can write. So fuck them."

When I look to the fish, there's an unfathomable sense of encouragement in the gentle way it floats.

An hour later, I want to let Cleo back in for an early dinner as revenge for giving me false hope.

"How could you do this to me?" I groan, my face buried into my hands, barely restraining myself from banging my head against the keyboard and making more and probably better progress than I've had since sitting down. "I trusted you!"

When I peek through my fingers to the screen where a blinking line cursor taunts me, barely having moved more than half a page from where it started, there's a new sense of dread to make good company with the lingering kind that's been in the pit of my stomach for the past couple of days.

"Can't you work with me, Fish? Give me something?" I ask, looking over to it. "You're being awfully selfish over there, honestly."

The fish, like all other creatures in the apartment, is silent. I shoot it a dry look.

"Can't write, apparently," I muse with a heavy, defeated sigh. "Can't write, can't be a successful adult, and can barely take care of a fucking fish. All right. Cool. Are take-backsies allowed, or did I miss my chance for that?"

There are zero answers given as Fish swims around in its little tank, the sprawling fins letting the water take it where it will. I roll my eyes. And everyone called me a freeloader.

"How do I even take care of a fish?" I ask myself out loud, for no other reason than it makes me feel a little less alone. And then, while I'm typing it in in the search bar, "How to take care of Betta fish?"

My inherent Google-savvy that's built into my millennial heart has me browsing a few wikiHow pages and as I take periodic glances over at Fish, my brows furrow, seriously disturbed. The more I scroll and scan, the more I wonder if maybe fish hell is really where I was going to end up.

"Oh my god, are you okay in there? Here I am, crying over some dude and you're basically dying in your own crap. Shit, Fish, I'm so sorry."

My eyes sweep over things like filter, thermostat and 5 gallon tank written across my screen, a complete juxtaposition to the small, round bowl that Fish is swimming in. Fish doesn't answer, but inside I assume it's crying.

At least that made the two of us. Misery loves company, and all that.

Clearing my throat and squaring my shoulder, I stand to my feet and point a sharp finger in Fish's direction. "Listen here, Fish. I'm going to be straight up with you."

Fish continues swimming, and I assume appreciates my candor.

"All of these things seem really expensive, and I am almost very incredibly broke, but you are my responsibility now and I can do this. I can keep you alive, and I'm going to get you some real ass plants because you are my friend and my friends deserve the best," I promise, stepping around my bed and reaching to swipe up my purse.

Cleo has returned and is poised in the doorway watching me. There's an unnatural sense of camaraderie for someone who is basically talking to themselves.

"When I get back with your new home, I'm going to finish writing that goddamn book, and I'm gonna send out some goddamn query letter to agents, because we are somebodies and we deserve it. Right Fish?"

When I pause for a response, I wait two seconds before immediately escaping the room because maybe getting outside and into the world of human interaction will be helpful in not sounding like a crazy person.

Still, a sense of renewal propels my steps forward, out from the elevator, through the lobby and onto the sidewalk. So much so, that when I see a familiar dark head of hair rounding the corner in front of me, an electric charge sparks down my spine. The reasonable part of me is reassuring that brown hair the chances of it being actually him are slim to none, and probably only an overactive figment of my imagination, but there's another part that whispers if I run fast enough I could probably catch up to him.

Just to check. Just to see. Just for peace of mind.

And I take a step forward, hand gripped tightly to my purse, heart dropped all the way down to the base of my spine and throbbing two beats too quick.

And then I take a step back, thinking of poor little Fish wasting away in its little tank, and turn, telling myself that Fish, and I, deserve better.

chapter twenty four

"VIKA, I DON'T THINK I can do this."

The carefully curated playlist featuring Destiny's Child and Outkast is barely drowning out Cecilia's barking on the phone about something with flowers, and Nat narrowly breaks over them. I heave a sigh, arm already aching from holding a lock of dark hair around the curling iron for over five seconds. "Listen, Nat, I can curl my hair just as good as any beauty school reject and I can do it for less than two hundred dollars. I get it's your wedding, but this is about the principle-"

"That's not-"

"Okay, it doesn't matter if she graduated, I'm using hyperbole. It's for effect. I'm a writer, you can't take away my poetic licence from me. I-"

"Vika, I can't do this."

I snort. "Dude, we tried on the dress yesterday, we already know it fits. I highly doubt 2AM McDonalds works that fast."

Without a snappy retort back, I pause. Shifting to gain a better look at her, I catch Nat's sharp green eyes softening in a way that takes me by surprise. She's chewing on the inside of her cheek and that spiral of panic she's rapidly and haphazardly tumbling into is written all over her face, exposed by the crease in her brow and the deep breath she takes. I blink to make sure my eyes aren't playing tricks on me.

A quick survey of the room and all the other bridesmaids are running around like worker bees with blinders on, too concerned with getting their false lashes and liquid lipstick just right to hear what Nat's saying. They're completely oblivious as she throws me another pleading look a la puppy dog left to starve in the rain.

"I'm going for a smoke," I announce to no one in particular, placing down the curling iron with my hair still half done. "Nat, come keep me company."

Natalya's already bunching up the edges of her dress between her fingers and making her way towards the balcony before I can even finish my sentence. Cecilia seems more concerned with me, though, from the way she freezes in place and wrinkles her nose.

"You're going to smell if you smoke," she says, somehow upping the nasal quality in her voice to new heights.

I wave her off, rolling my eyes. "I'll buy a breath mint, Cici."

The pet name isn't coming from a particularly affectionate place, but she sends a glimpse of camaraderie from across the room that I can only awkwardly return with a sheepish grin before disappearing out the balcony.

Nat's leaning against the railing, picturesque with the mid-July sunlight reflecting off her blonde hair pulled into a loose updo. Despite the mermaid-style ivory dress she's swathed in, her eyes staring off into the distance aren't screaming wedding bells.

"If you're here to announce your true love for me, you're late. I've already taken a vow of celibacy in honour of Remington," I say, grinning, as I slide up next to her.

Her brows knit. "Isn't that your fish?"

"He is my child, Nat. How dare you? Remington is not just a fish."

She opens her mouth as if to make a snappy reply, but instead of words only a troubled sigh falls through. There's an unmistakable sag to her shoulders, and although wedding dresses are basically anvils wrapped up in rhinestones, it's clear it runs deeper than that.

"Hey, seriously, what's up?" I ask, softer than before, gently nudging her with my shoulder.

There's a beat of quiet, the sounds of the city barely touching us from up here. She sniffs, picking at her cuticles, refusing to look me in the eye.

"Am I making the right decision?"

There's a second of processing. "What do you mean? Are you making the right decision in marrying Mark?" I blink, barely believing the words coming out of my mouth.

"I'm only twenty-five," she says, in a voice that sounds more like my own than Nat's. "Carrie didn't get married until she was 40. Am I honestly ready to make this life-altering decision at twenty-five?"

"Carrie?" I pause, narrowing my eyes in suspicion. "As in- Carrie Bradshaw? What did I say about making life decisions based on Sex and the City? No! Bad! No bueno! I didn't watch enough of that show to make a strong enough case why this is a bad idea, but I'm the queen of bad ideas I know a bad idea when I see one!"

Her nose wrinkles. "Isn't that what you've been saying this entire time, though? That I'm too young for this, that I'm jumping head-first into this without really thinking it through?"

There's a moment where the entire Dr. Phil spiel evaporates from my tongue, when I meet her eyes to find them shining, just a soft suggestion of the conflict lingering behind. It's cold and unforgiving on the back of my neck, a replay of all the doubt I've sown over the past year, flippant comments here, rolling my eyes there, all meandering to come to the single point on this balcony.

I draw a deep breath.

"Listen, if we've learned anything the past couple of months, it's that I literally don't know anything, and every statement I've ever made is anywhere between ten to a hundred percent false," I say with a wide gesture of my arm as if all my poor decisions were laid out in front of us, although I don't think a single skyline could carry them all. "I've been talking out of my ass so much it's almost presidential."

She snorts, but it's half-hearted and there's still the ever-present threat of tears in her eyes. "Okay, but-"

"But what? Are you saying that I was also right when I said that green wasn't your colour?"

She scoffs. "That's different, I'm obviously a spring."

"And not even two weeks ago, when I was banging my head against my keyboard saying I was never going to be a real author, who convinced me to get off my ass and finish editing my book, and send out not one, but multiple query letters to agents?"

She hesitates, bites her lips and then, softly, "I did."

"And who said I couldn't take care of a fish?"

She cocks a brow. "You did?"

"And guess what? He's still swimming! Remington's doing great! I mean, I think. I can't really tell, because he's a fish, but damn fucking straight he's still alive," I beam and grab her hand, warm and freshly manicured, but still trembling.

"I don't get what your point is?" she says, but lets her hand slip into mine naturally. "This about Mark and I. And a wedding. That's happening in an hour. And changing my life forever."

I shoot her a knowing look, brows raised, mouth pursed. "My point still stands. I'm an idiot, and I don't know anything other than I love you, and that I would snatch you up and run off into the sunset in a heartbeat if you said the word."

She swallows. "And?"

"And you haven't said that. Look, I think Mark is great, and it's not only a money thing, I swear." She fixes me with a dry look. "It's not! I'm quite possibly one of the most selfish people in existence, and I would love to have you single and ready to mingle, believe me, but you love Mark, don't you?"

Nat draws a deep breath, shaky and sure. "I do, Vi, of course I do. I've loved him more than I've loved anyone, but, I mean..."

"But what?" I push.

"But what if it doesn't work out? What if he decides he wants something else later? What if I'm not what he wants anymore, or the other way around?"

She's chewing on her bottom lip, a habit that's all too familiar after years and years of learning her patterns like my own. I can tell it's the only thing that's holding back the tears pooling in her eyes, just moments from breaking over the precipice, and she squeezes my hand like a buoy in an unforgiving ocean. My throat tightens when I meet her eyes.

"Then he'd be a bigger idiot than me, but I don't think he is, Nat."

There's another moment of silence, and then Nat's blowing out a controlled breath, waving with her free hand at her eyes and aggressively staring up into the sky. "This is going to ruin my makeup, stop being such a goddamn Hallmark card, who are you and what have you done with my best friend?"

I snort, grinning, and give her hand a tight squeeze before letting go. "I'm a fish mother now, I'm a brand new person."

She laughs too, sharp and loud, still frantically trying to neutralize the tears.

"Are you sure you want to do this?" I ask her with a pointed look, drinking in her rouged cheeks and wine red lips, reading every micro-expression on her face. "I just want whatever makes you happy."

She nods again, and a watery smile flashes across her face. "Oh god, more than anything. Honestly, I can't picture my life without him.

I'm just scared, but I want this. I think it's going to be the most nerve-wracking but the most worth risk of my life."

I can't help but feel a twinge of jealousy at the flash flood of affection in her eyes, so transparent I can see straight into her heart. But it's small, and it's easily overpowered by the heartwarming contentment knowing that she deserves it and so much more. A small smile slips onto my face.

"Then stop crying! You paid way too much money to be ruining your eyeliner!" I bump her with my arm. "It's one thing to be rich, it's another to be wasteful. I will not be a maid of honour to an ugly bride."

"Bitch, I look beautiful in whatever my makeup looks like," she says, wiping her nose with her knuckle and clicking her tongue. "And if you want, you don't, well, you don't have to be my maid of honour. Cecilia can take that."

My head shoots back, eyes narrowed suspiciously. "Excuse you, over my dead body. I have not been your friend for over 15 years to not be your maid of honour. I've put time into this, I've put in effort, how dare you?"

She rolls her eyes, waving me off. "I don't mean it like that, obviously. If you want to, the title's all yours. I just mean if you didn't want to, you know, walk down the aisle with Noel or whatever. I mean, I could convince Mark to switch but-"

I raise a hand to interrupt, brow arched. "Weren't you the one that said I had to pay for my own mistakes? I had to deal with the cleanup?"

"That may have been some unnecessary old couple meddling on Mark and I's part. You guys aren't teenagers, and I don't think anyone expected it to turn out how it did." She shrugs sheepishly.

I crinkle my nose, turning back to the city. "I could literally have my legs chewed off by a rabid pack of chihuahuas, and I would still drag my body down that aisle. Noel's nobody to stop me."

It's weird to say his name out loud again, after running it over and over in my head for so long but never giving it any true breath. It rolls off the tongue in an achingly familiar way, but lingers in the air with a heartbreaking note that's still hard to swallow. His face flashes, dark eyes set behind those thick rimmed frames, and I ignore the tightness of my chest.

She pauses for a moment, searching my face with earnest, but doesn't push it further, thankfully. Instead, her arms wrap around me and then she's burying her face in my shoulder, squeezing me so tightly I'm rocked off-balance. I take a moment to return the hug, but it's warm, and it's soft and it's just right. The touch starvation doesn't settle in until I'm swallowed up by her presence, and I have to take a moment to fight back my own tears, because I've already done my makeup too.

When I break away, I've composed myself enough to shoot her a genuine enough grin. "Now, in consideration with what I said before, I'm not totally convinced that the moon landing isn't fake-"

"I do not have time to tell you how wrong you so very, very much are, I'm getting married! Shut up and help me fix my false lashes."

The other bridesmaids barely notice as we enter back inside, other than Cecilia, who's already throwing a can of Febreeze at me with more force than I personally think is necessary. Between the mimosas and the liquid lipstick touch ups, it barely feels like five minutes before we're all shuffling about in the back of the church, smoothing down our hair and bubbling over with nervous energy.

When Nat pulls my hand in hers, there's a grounded sensation that overwhelms me for the second time that day, and she shoots me a small smile that's an instant Xanax to my nerves. It's only a few seconds later when she squeezes my hand and looks passed me, I realize the full extent to her move.

The groom's men are all dressed to the nines in their sleek, charcoal grey suits, baby pink ties and Italian leather shoes. Mark's fresh-faced brother is all smiles as usual, and he's immediately drowning Nat in compliments from the moment he sees her, the Vanderbilt family charm. Alexei, Mark's old roommate, gives me a small smile and nod of acknowledgement, which I return the best I can with my heart beating a tattoo against my chest.

Trailing just behind the group is the one person I'd been both dreading and anticipating for days, tousled dark hair slicked back and beard trimmed to expose the sharpness of his jaw I know all too well. His hands are tucked into his pockets, his face downcast. As if feeling my intense gaze drilling holes into him, he looks up.

With my nerves all bundled in my throat, I squeeze Nat's hand back as a reminder to breathe again.

Every single emotion I'd been shoving deep down to regain some semblance of my regular life immediately betrays me, and I have to draw a breath to settle my tripping pulse. As the planner begins to order us all in line, Nat's hand slips from mine, and I'm alone.

It's his cologne that meets me before he ever does, tortuously reliable notes of fresh mint and sharp citrus. My eyes have fallen down to my feet, and soon another pair are crowding into my line of view, black and accentuated with traditional broguing.

When I force my gaze up to meet his, his dark eyes threaten to disarm me completely.

"How're you?" Noel asks, small, unsure. He toys with his tie, even though it's already laid perfectly against his chest.

Nat's protective presence is still at my back, but I square my shoulders and set my eyes forward. "I'm splendid, thanks." My tone's sharp, unforgiving, an arctic breeze passing through every syllable.

He nods, swallowing in a way I can trace with his Adam's apple against his throat. There's another beat of quiet.

"You look very nice."

"I know."

His gaze runs over my profile, down the dip of my nose and over my heated cheeks, combing through for something more substantial, but I'm not so generous. As the doors open and a wave of moment turns to attention, everyone's excited eyes just waiting for a glimpse of the blushing bride, I silently lock my arms with his.

Noel doesn't say anything, and despite the crestfallen turn of his mouth I catch in my peripherals, I don't say anything either. The thick quiet that's deafening between us is settled throughout the nuptials and wedding photos, a constant orbiting around each other but never quite breaking each other's atmosphere. I'm both ignoring his and Nat's longing stares, and distract myself with the ever-present flute of champagne in my hand.

Unfortunately, there's barely a buzz by the time I'm tucked in the back corner of the room, the reception already unravelling to new heights in front of and without me. I'm sucking on the end of a steak skewer, chin tucked in my palm and elbow resting on the table as I listen to Nat's grandpa's never-ending voice, unsure whether this is all the same home country story or multiple that I hadn't caught the beginning and ends of.

It's with an undeniable flicker of jealousy as I see Cecilia throwing her head back and laughing as she tries to do a shimmy on the dance floor. I can shimmy so much better than her.

"And, you won't believe, bear, huge bear, size of full tree bear appear right in front of me! I, twelve years old, you won't believe, I stare into the eye of bear and say, I say-"

The old, heavily accented man's elaborate hand gestures are interrupted as a hand taps gently on his shoulder. His forehead wrinkles deepen with a frown as he turns, and my entire body seizes up.

Noel pauses, and my pulse forgets a beat. His eyes are dark brown and earnest, searching for something in mine as he takes a deep breath.

"My apologies for the interruption. Can we talk?"

the end

"APOLOGY NOT ACCEPTED, and no."

There's a flash of hurt across Noel's face. "Is there anything I can say?"

Mr. Mikhailov opens his mouth to answer, but I'm faster. "We're clearly in the middle of something," I snap. "I understand basic human decency might be below your pay grade, but if you could allow us to continue our conversation, that would be great."

I shoot him a heartless smile, taking another sip of my whiskey sour.

He stumbles, and I should feel triumphant at the lost look in his eyes, but it's empty. The reservoir of outrage I've been consistently dipping into when confronted with Noel isn't as roaring as it first came to be. The victory is short-lived, and my gaze falls to the table, unable to swallow any of the emotion that's drowning in his eyes.

"Okay," he says, but the tone is his voice betrays he's anything but. "I'm sorry, I'll leave."

Just as he's ducked his head and turned on his heel, Mr. Mikhailov's loyalty that I'd thought we'd clearly established is ruthlessly broken.

"What you mean? Come, come, sit, listen!" the old man cries out with a grin plastered across his face, arms waving Noel to the seat next to him. "More is merry!"

I knew there was a reason Russians were always the villains in movies.

There's a quick pause where Noel and I lock eyes, the entire world at a stand-still, silently asking questions I don't have the answers to. Nat's grandpa is giving a Santa-esque belly laugh, still patting the seat next to him.

I give a defeated sigh.

"Well," I say, gesturing to the seat. "Don't be rude, the man told you to sit."

The hesitance on Noel's face is almost palpable, eyes wide and dumbfounded, body half-turned and unsure. I have to give another nod towards the seat to get him to move again, and he's slow on the uptake. He watches me the entire time, as if waiting for me to chuck my drink directly at his face, but I turn back to Nat's grandpa with a deep inhale instead.

Mr. Mikhailov doesn't seem bothered at all by the uncomfortable atmosphere that's settled over the table and continues regaling his epic tale of Russian Man vs. Russian Bear with the drunk enthusiasm of multiple vodka shots. I'm keeping a steady stare, refusing to acknowledge the pair of dark eyes burning into me, mostly because I'm not sure what else to say.

Noel's confusion is directly reflected in the dangerous swirl of emotions taking a hold in my throat. The anger has faded, leaving something in its wake I can't quite make sense of. Forming coherent words to explain to Noel seems like a lost cause as I absently toy with the skewer on my plate, not even sure why I even want to in the first place.

Nat shoots me a concerned look from across the room, but I send back a comforting smile. I'm not even sure what I'm comforting about.

I'm begrudgingly impressed that Noel doesn't move for the next half hour, even entertaining Nat's grandpa with a few well-placed nods and questions. I've noted that his sister, Angelica, is entertained with Christian somewhere else in the room. Nat's looks of concern aren't going unnoticed.

Noel and I, on the other hand, have gotten into the terrible middle school habit of staring at one other, accidentally locking eyes and then quickly looking away just as quick. I'm spinning the straw of my empty whiskey sour, but I don't move to get another.

In fact, the only thing that brings pause to Mr. Mikhailov is a hand on the old man's shoulder, cutting him off mid-sentence. "What? What is it?"

Nat's dad is standing behind, familiar with his prominent, pinched nose and crows feet, a proverbial warmth in his light green eyes. "Papa, let me introduce you to someone, you can finish your story with Victoria and Noel later. Come, come."

"Ah!" I protest, hand in mid-air. "It's fine, I, uh, Nat and I discussed this. This is totally okay, don't worry." I reassure him with a small smile.

The salt and peppered man shoots me a sly look, winking. "It's okay, you kids have fun." Without another word, he's then whisking the old man away, only leaving the empty vodka glass in his wake.

I pause for a moment, drinking in the scene of Noel and I, now alone at the table. His jaw is twitching, and he's looking down, concentrated on his fingers tapping against his whiskey glass. The battle of his thoughts is betrayed by the crease of his brow, or that could be wishful thinking.

Pushing myself off the table, I sigh.

"Alright, congratulations, you've earned yourself five minutes. Let's go outside."

Noel blinks. "Are you sure? If you don't want to, I-"

"I wouldn't have asked if I didn't mean it, Noel," I say, swallowing down the nerves collected in my throat, and gesture for him to stand. "I know publicity isn't your thing, so let's take this outside."

His brows furrow. "I-"

"Outside," I cut him off, turning my back.

It's with quick, long strides I cross the room, and there's a building anticipation in my veins as I push open the back door. Outside is a quintessential July night, balmy and humid, a stickiness already clinging to the nape of my neck. A weak breeze toys with the edges of my peach chiffon dress. I rest my back against the brick building.

Noel is quick to follow me, and there's only a few selfish moments before he's joining me with the distant sound of crickets and rustling of leaves. When our eyes meet, he stops.

I'm so easily swallowed up by the whirlwind of his gaze, it takes a moment for me to find my footing again.

"What do you want, Noel?" I ask, and I can't temper the exhausted notes in my voice.

Tired of him or tired of pretending, that I can't decide on. The way that my pulse trips when I look him in the eyes betrays me.

"First, I wanted to apologize for showing up at your work- that was, I was being inconsiderate. I didn't think that through. I didn't know where else to go, but that wasn't right. I'm sorry." He's carding his hand through his hair, gaze flickering from me to the asphalt and back again. "I'm sorry."

I cross my arms over my chest. "Look Noel- it's fine. Don't worry about it. Let's just leave this be, okay?" I say, ignoring the bitter taste in my mouth. "We agreed on that, didn't we? That this was supposed to be over with anyway? No need to drag it out."

"Vika, I'm sorry, but I can't pretend that I want that," he says, and then pauses, swallowing. "If you don't want this- if that's what you want, I'll walk away. But you have to know that I never thought this would end tonight." He takes a step forward, eyes pursuing after mine. "I know that I did this wrong, I know I should've done this better, taken you out properly, the way you deserved."

"I don't care about that, I don't need to be taken out."

Another step closer, and my breath hitches in my throat.

"But I wanted to- want to. I want this. I want," he falters, then, "you."

The word hangs in the air for a moment, and it's aching in the way that it falls heavy on my chest, seeping through my skin, burning up.

"No," I shake my head, ignoring the heat behind my lashes. "No, Noel, you don't. You want parts of me. And I can't do that. If we're not pretending, let's not pretend like we both don't know that this is, we're not- what I want is to be treated with respect."

His mouth twitches in a frown. "I never meant to treat you without respect, Vika, I-"

"I know that I'm fucked up," I continue, ignoring him. "And I'm brash, and literally the definition of classless. I know I'm not the girl you bring home to your parents, okay? I know that, but I'm not going to let you make me feel bad about it, because I don't, Noel. And I don't want to."

My hands have tightened to fists at my side, and there's a winded quality to my breath even though I've barely moved. My tongue is finally lighter without the weight of those words hovering behind my teeth. Noel's eyes are shining under the pale moonlight, dark and searching, a frown marked on his face.

He opens his mouth for a moment, rests a hand on his forehead, and then sighs.

"I never, Vika, I'm so sorry. I never wanted you to feel that way."

"This isn't only one throwaway comment, Noel. And you know that."

"I know," he admits, voice soft, teeming with emotion I can't decipher in the night air. "Those times, Christian's birthday, all of that. It was never about you, I just want you to know that. My family's, they're... complicated."

My lips thin. "And I'm too simple to understand that?"

"No! No, that's not it." His eyes widen a fraction. "That's not it at all. I mean complicated, as in its a lot. I didn't want to bother you with it."

His Adam's apple dips dangerously in his throat, eyes falling to the ground.

I arch a brow, arms folded over my chest. "Baggage? You don't want to involve me in your baggage, that's what you're going with?"

"It's a lot to deal with. I don't expect anyone to deal with it, you especially. You shouldn't have to."

The vulnerability that's captivated his face is a swift punch in the stomach, all sorts of heart strings I never knew I had being torn apart before I can get a better grip on them. I shift in my spot to stop myself from crossing the distance between us. Every vein simultaneously ignites and collapses in my body.

"I'm the queen of baggage," I murmur.

There's another flood of quiet between us, and from the way Noel's jaw twitches, the tender sigh that falls from his lips, I can tell he's hunting for the right words. The pale light of the moon could be a lie, but it's softening all his features in a way that's exposing him more than I've ever seen, defenceless in a way I've never gotten close to.

"Did you mean it?" I finally ask, brows furrowed. "When you said that you didn't want this to end tonight?"

There's a small, sad smile on his face. "I think my biggest mistake was somehow letting you think I wanted anything else. I'm not even sure how you don't know that I think you're amazing."

"Amazing?" I echo.

He takes another step forward, and now we're close, in a way that earlier today we'd barely brushed the surface of. He reaches out a hand, breaths away from my cupping my cheek, and I freeze, but he drops it before impact.

"I've never met anyone who has managed to drag me so far out of my comfort zone, while also making me feel so... right, at the same time. It shouldn't make sense, you don't make sense, but I'd do anything to feel that way again."

A shiver trickles down my spine. "I mean, I just made you try Chinese food."

"There's nothing more I want to do than eat your garbage food and watch your garbage TV with you."

I can't help the small laugh that escapes me. His eyes light up in a way I haven't seen all night. It threatens to swipe the solid ground right from underneath me, but there's still something inside of me that's holding on tightly to the edge of the cliff, digging my fingers into the dirt, refusing to let go just yet.

"I won't be some dirty little secret, Noel. I want more than that, and I deserve better than that," I say, a quiet gravity in my voice.

"You do, and more than anything, I want to give that to you."

We lock eyes again, and my palms are going sweaty. The tight hold is beginning to slip through my fingers.

"I don't love you, Vika."

I snort. "Please, don't overwhelm me all at once."

He smiles, small, scratching at the back of his neck. "I'm not going to say I do yet, it's not easy for me with that kind of thing. And I'm warning you, before we get any farther with this, but I can honestly say that I could. I really could. And that terrifies me, but I want to follow that through more than anything."

There's an inexplicable warmth in my chest, slowly melting away all the weight that's set a semi-permanent residence over the course of the last few weeks. His words are like velvet against my bare shoulders in the night air.

"And Cleopatra?" I ask, brows raised.

He knits his brows. "What about her?"

"What if we don't get her blessing?" I take a step closer, so now we're toe-to-toe, and I can help the grin curving on my face.

He looks genuinely conflicted for a moment, mouth dipping into a frown, a crease on his forehead, the hesitance written all over his face. "Well, you haven't learned how to brush her correctly. If I just showed you, I know she'd-"

And then I let go.

It's with one swift movement, I'm reaching up and smothering the rest of his thought with my lips, pressing them against his with a quick, chaste kiss. He blinks in confusion for a moment, as if it still hasn't all set in yet, and then he's chasing my mouth with his. I'm smiling into the kiss as I wrap my arms around his neck and pull him closer, the warmth of his body no contest to the heat that's unfurling inside of me, a consequence of the friction of his words all collecting together and igniting in an inextinguishable fire.

He pulls away first, breath coming in soft pants, forehead pressing against mine. "I promise I'm going to make it up to you."

I grin. "I promise that I'll let you."

And then I'm cupping the back of his head and capturing his lips with mine once more, intoxicated more with his taste than any champagne I've drunk all night. Even though they're only words, I want to believe him more than anything, believe in the genuine notes I hope are reflected in those coffee dark eyes of his, in the slight stumble of his words and the red dusting of his cheeks. The man I'd uncovered in Mark's apartment is underneath the black tie and thick frames, kissing me back under the night sky, just as dizzy as I am.

As I'm running my hands down his torso, all achingly familiar in a way I'd never thought I'd touch again, he's pressing a quick kiss on my forehead.

"We should go back inside, while I'd love to stay out here and kiss you all night, I think you've missed enough of Nat's wedding," he says, voice barely breaking above a whisper and rough in a way that resonates all the way into my bones.

I sigh, but for the first time, my shoulders aren't heavy. "I guess you're right, this one time. Let's go."

When I pull away from his embrace, pushing off from his chest, it's cold in ways that's aren't right. The door to the hall is a few feet away, but someone it feels as if it exists in an entirely different reality than the one we're steeped in, filled with an entire world of consequences that can't touch us out here.

"Wait," he says, and my pulse trips. "One second."

I turn slowly, my entire heart hanging in the balance. "What?"

"Is there anything else I can do to begin making this up to you?"

The relief crashes down onto me in an overwhelmingly comforting wave, and I let out a breath I hadn't realized I was holding. It takes everything inside of me not to press him against the brick wall and rain kisses all over his face, and instead I grin at him. "Ten thousand dollars?"

His eyes widen. "What?"

It's only for a moment, and then I'm completely betraying any straight face, erupting into laughter. Noel visibly relaxes, a small, knowing smile curving on his lips.

"A dance would be nice," I admit, honestly, and hold out my hand in a way that's devastatingly vulnerable.

His hand slips into mine naturally, beaming, and then presses a small kiss against my temple. "Christ, I have no idea when I became so smitten with you."

I snort, squeezing his hand. "Smitten? You're such a fucking dork."

There's a beat of quiet, and Noel doesn't say anything, only looks away. I feel that last heartstring in my very depths tugged down to my very core.

"And I'm pretty smitten with you too," I follow up, leaning up on my tiptoes for another kiss.

When I pull away, Noel's smile is so genuine, it winds me on an entirely new level.

As we step in sync towards the door, I know we're only breaths from breaking the spell of moonlight and cricket symphony. On the other side is the reality of our jobs, of our families and our friends, the weight of the world ready to drop on our shoulders the moment we step through the threshold.

But for some reason, with the warmth of his palm in my own, it doesn't feel that scary.

***

WE'RE HERE. WE DID IT. WE'VE MADE IT. THE END HAS COME. WOW.

I just want to say, thank you guys so much for reading Vika and Noel's story to the end. It honestly means so much to me that you guys actually take the time to read it until the end!

I think that's all for now, so this will be the last trash goblin out. THANK YOU GUYS SO MUCH AGAIN! LOVE YOU GUYS!

CPSIA information can be obtained
at www.ICGtesting.com
Printed in the USA
LVHW081538170323
741847LV00015B/833

9 781805 099222